# *What the critics are saying...*

*Naughty Mistress Nita*

"...an arresting romance of intense, spine tingling ardor. Naughty Mistress Nita pulses with eroticism, sensuality, and breath taking sex." ~ *Fallen Angel Reviews*

"A steamy, erotic read. The love scenes are captivating and sensual. This is the perfect read for anyone looking to turn up the heat and indulge in something "naughty." ~ *Sizzling Romances*

"Sizzling hot, naughty and impossible to put down... This is one hot and quick read that pulls one in and overrides the senses." ~ *The Road to Romance*

"...a wonderful, passionate, and humorous novel with great characters...I was wrapped up from page one. You don't want to miss this one." ~ *Sensual Romance Reviews*

"A tale of desire and romance...Naughty Mistress Nita awakens hidden desires in the most reluctant of readers. You will not be disappointed!" ~ *Love Romances*

"A delightful tale of what one will do when faced with the unexpected and the desire to just let it all hang out... If you are looking for a story that has some spanking and light bondage and a fairly quick read then pick up Naughty Mistress Nita, you will not be disappointed." ~ *A Romance Review*

## Lessons in Lust Major

"Tawny Taylor's Lessons in Lust Major is a delightful weekend romp full of sizzling fun. Get ready for a teacher's conference that will leave you laughing out loud while you're melting in your chair." ~ *eCataRomance Reviews*

"Tawny Taylor has done it again with a story of finding love in unlikely places; I will definitely be on the lookout for more of her work in the future." ~ *Just Erotic Romance Reviews*

"*LESSONS IN LUST MAJOR* builds the reader into a fever pitch of desire filled with sexual tension and then delivers the gratification with such gusto that it will take your breath away." ~ *Sizzling Romances*

## Sexual Healing

"Sensual and riveting, Sexual Healing is a contagious read from the first page. It is impossible to not get caught up in the banter and foreplay between the highly likeable characters." ~ *Coffee Time Romance*

"Ms. Taylor certainly has panache for HOT, romantic comedy. SEXUAL HEALING is exactly what the doctor prescribes for a fun, sexy and remarkable romp." ~ *eCataRomance Reviews*

"Anyone looking for a delightful love story with tenderness and impassioned encounters should pick up a copy of Sexual Healing." ~ *Just Erotic Romance Reviews*

# Behind
# CLOSED DOORS

Jodi Lynn Copeland
Tawny Taylor

ELLORA'S CAVE
ROMANTICA PUBLISHING

An Ellora's Cave Romantica Publication

www.ellorascave.com

Behind Closed Doors

ISBN 1419953818
ALL RIGHTS RESERVED.
Naughty Mistress Nita Copyright © 2003 Jodi Lynn Copeland
Lessons in Lust Major Copyright © 2004 Tawny Taylor
Sexual Healing Copyright © 2005 Tawny Taylor

Edited by Pamela Campbell, Sue-Ellen Gower, Martha Punches
Cover art by Syneca

Trade paperback Publication August 2006

Excerpt from *About Monday* Copyright © Sydney Laine Allan, 2006

# Contents

# NAUGHTY MISTRESS NITA

*By Jodi Lynn Copeland*

ഔ

# Dedication

ತಾ

*To all the "Naughty Nitas" of the world.*
*May your walk on the wild side be as rewarding as Anita's.*

# Chapter One

### ဆ

Jordan was dead.

At least she would be when Anita Roemer got her hands on her. Her so-called best friend had contacted her in major panic mode this morning, with a request no one in their right mind would have agreed to.

'Meet my appointment for me and tell him I can't make it,' Jordan had said. 'I've tried calling, but there's no answer. He's prepaid and I can't just leave him hanging.'

Meet her appointment, Anita thought now with a snort, easier said than done considering Jordan worked as a professional dominatrix. Not to mention this particular appointment was nowhere near to Jordan's office, but in a tiny cabin nestled so deeply in the Picanti Mountains no one would've guessed it even existed.

And as far as being in her right mind, clearly Anita wasn't, since at this very moment she stood knocking on the hardwood door of that particular secluded cabin. Worse than lost marbles, and the reason she was going to ring Jordan's neck, was the appointment in question didn't even appear to be around.

She'd committed a major transgression—at least for her anyway—and driven the forty-mile trip ten miles over the limit to make it here on schedule. And for what, to spend her time knocking on the door of an empty cabin while the gods of thunder streamed non-stop insults around her?

She should leave right now. She had far better things to do with her Friday evening than stand here knocking away. Cleaning needed to be done...or arranging her bookcase...or, well, she could always pay that visit to her parents she'd been putting off for too long now. Only what if Jordan got in trouble because of it? Worse, what if her friend thought she'd never made the trip in the first place, and tossed out another remark like the one she'd flung at her earlier today. The one that pushed Anita over the edge and made her agree to come to this ramshackle shed in the middle of nowhere.

Jordan's words burned through her mind even now. *"If you aren't up to telling him I can't make it, you can always be my stand in."* And then she'd laughed loud and long.

Was it really so hard to imagine Anita letting loose enough to make a man her slave? Yes, she was uptight at times. Maybe even a bit on the prim and proper side. Certainly as uniform and statistical as the balance sheets she handled through her job at the accounting firm. All of those things were a direct result of her stern upbringing. None of those things meant she couldn't control a man, bend him to her every whim.

Her sexual exploits might be limited to two very tidy, organized sessions of standard missionary-style sex, but that wasn't because she was following in her mother's goody-two-shoes footsteps. Or that her minister father's numerous sermons about premarital sex being sinful had convinced her to abstain. It was merely because she had yet to find someone she cared to go a second round with, let alone experiment with outside the norm.

At twenty-five she was still plenty young. If and when a man came along who revved her engine in all the right ways, then she'd cut loose and try all those things she'd dared to fantasize about. Until then, she was fine and dandy with her conservative ways.

A loud rumbling shook Anita from her musings. Through the dense canvas of elm, pine and sycamore trees, she peered warily at the dark, roiling sky. Hitching her purse strap higher on her shoulder, she breathed in the unmistakable scent of the forthcoming storm mingled with the forest greenery. For Jordan's sake, she'd wait a few more minutes. Either that or until the rain gods decided to join forces with the thunder gods.

Less than a minute had passed when, with an ominous hiss, the sky opened up. Cold, hard rain pelted down, instantly soaking her through to the skin. Expelling a rare curse, Anita twisted the cabin's doorknob. It turned in her hand, the door pushing inward. She dashed into the building's warmth, closed the door behind her, and turned to face the room. Her breath caught as she took in the cabin—make that, pigsty—before her.

"Good gracious, the man's a slob."

How could anyone live like this? Clothes lay strewn across the faded couch and recliner that centered the small building's sitting room. Several books were tossed about on the scarred coffee table and the T.V. was on!

Who on earth would go away and leave the T.V. on? Unless he was home.

Anita shook the excess rainwater from her hair and sweater and then opened her purse to the business card section. She pulled out the card Jordan had handed her earlier that morning. Zane Matthews was emblazoned on the card's front in brilliant gold. She stifled a laugh at his title—architect. Maybe that explained how he managed to stack his clothes so high without fearing they'd topple.

"Mr. Matthews?" she called out, weaving her way through the chaos and into the only other room aside from the bathroom—a good-sized bedroom in nearly the same appalling state as the main room.

Crinkling her nose, she called his name again. Still no answer.

Dang. She couldn't stand around all day waiting for him. Just a few more minutes, she promised herself again. Until then she'd do a little straightening. Whoever the guy was he'd surely appreciate some tidying. And maybe her selfless efforts would help smooth things over when he realized she'd entered his home without permission.

Forty-five minutes and one moderately clean cabin later, Anita had had enough. Her back was sore, her feet hurt and darn she was tired. The big, pine-framed bed called to her from the corner of the bedroom, and it was all she could do to stop from whimpering. She could test it out, make sure she'd gotten the corners tight enough when she'd made it. After all, she'd hate to think she was doing something halfway.

"Just a quick test," she murmured as she lay down on the soft, forest-themed comforter and inhaled the mixed aroma of man and pine.

She'd get up in a second...or maybe two, she thought fleetingly as her eyes drifted closed. Or three. Really, what was her hurry anyway, all she had waiting for her at home was more work. Four minutes and then she was really, really going to get up.

\* \* \* \* \*

"Son of a bitch," Zane Matthews vented as he yanked off his sopping wet flannel shirt and tossed it onto the hardwood bedroom floor.

It wasn't enough the fish weren't biting, or that he'd gotten stuck in the worst thunderstorm to hit the Picanti Mountain range this spring, subsequently drenching every inch of him during his trek back from the lake to his temporary home. But now he had to find a goddamned woman in his bed! A woman whose services he'd flatly refused each and every time his buddies suggested he spend a little time at her hands.

He didn't need a fucking dominatrix or whatever the p.c. term was for the short-haired brunette sprawled face down and snoring like a banshee on his bed. He was doing just fine getting past Trina's deceit all on his own.

Worse than his so-called friends setting him up with the trespassing she-devil was the fact she'd touched his stuff. It had taken most of last week to get it arranged so the place felt more like a home and less like a temporary residence until the paperwork on his divorce was final. Now the place was neat as a pin, and smelled like...he inhaled harshly and grunted. It smelled like flowers of all the damned things!

She had to go, and now.

"Pardon me, princess, but nap time's over," Zane bit out in a voice to rival the thunder that roared outside the cabin.

She remained still, her arms in a death-grip around his pillow and her snoring ceaseless. He tromped to the bedside and grabbed her shoulder, shaking it.

"I said, nap time's over. Now get up and get out, unless you want me to remove you myself." He bit back a groan. What the hell kind of offer was that? With her profession she'd likely revel in bodily removal. Especially if brute force were involved.

The brunette remained immobile, lifeless, aside from the subtle rise and fall of her chest with her breathing. Zane rolled her over, more than ready to pick her up and toss her out his front door. He paused as her face came into view—creamy skin clean of makeup, eyes that held no mascara, and a turned up freckled nose. He took quick stock of her clothes—beige slacks and a coral knit sweater—and smirked.

This little scrap of nothing was supposed to beat him into submission? More like convince him to join a monastery. A nun, that's what she looked like with her small, oval face, pixie hair cut, and conservative attire. It'd almost be worth it to let her have her way with him, just to see what kind of commands she'd dole out in her voice that was undoubtedly soft and gentle as a mouse. Almost.

Nun or nympho she was on her way out.

Slipping his arms beneath her, Zane hefted her against him. She didn't weigh much, but she definitely had some curves to her compact body. Her bulky sweater hid them, but his hand could tell a hell of a lot from a subtle brush. So could his cock, which apparently just remembered how long it had been since he'd indulged in sex.

Real fucking nice. An accidental scrape of his hand over Sleeping Beauty's breasts and he was rock hard and raring to go. Only he wasn't going. She was.

He started for the door, stopping abruptly when her arm came up and snaked around his neck. She nuzzled against the muscles of his damp, naked chest, her soft, tousled curls teasingly erotic. His nipples hardened with the silky swipe of her tresses, and his balls drew tight at the unexpected and way-too-intimate gesture.

Shit, he didn't need this—his body working against him. And hell, did she have to smell so good? Maybe it wasn't his place that smelled like flowers, maybe she did.

He buried his nose in her short, sable hair and drew in a long, testosterone spurring breath. Faint lavender filled his nostrils and heated his blood. His cock pulsed, making its hunger known, as the bulk of that blood drained from his head straight to his groin.

Maybe he should take advantage of her presence after all. Not let her beat the shit out of him, or whatever it was dominatrices did, but a little mutual sex, some one on one fun. The wild and crazy kind Trina flatly refused to engage in—with him anyway. She didn't have a single problem fucking every which way but Sunday with her coworker turned overnight lover. Too bad the night in question was a year before and Zane hadn't discovered the truth until a few months back.

Fuck it, he thought, resting his gaze on the rising swell of the pretty little stranger's breasts, why not? She was paid for and the guys wouldn't buy him a two-bit hooker. They said she was certified and everything. And really, who had to know he'd given in?

* * * * *

"Oh, yes, don't stop!"

Don't wake up was more like it. If this dream ended before Anita climaxed there was going to be some real heck to pay. The macho man stroking his tongue over her bared, aching breasts wasn't her usual type—way too rugged with his scratchy beard and overlong hair—but he sure knew what he was doing.

His rough hands moved to her slacks, quickly tugging down the zipper and yanking on the belt hoops until the pants rode low at her hips. He slid his hand past the wide vee of the zipper and stroked her slick feminine flesh through her low cut electric red and midnight black silk panties—the outrageous shade and heavenly texture her lone indulgence in the wilder side of life. One big, callused finger moved past the thin cotton material, and she bucked up hard against him as he petted her swollen, juicy clit.

"Is that where it hurts, princess?" His raw voice abraded her senses, sent her mind whirling with sensation after sensation along with the help of his continuously probing finger. Around them, the air crackled with currents as hot and unending as the storm that wailed at the fringes of her mind.

A second finger joined the first and Anita blocked out the flashes of light to concentrate completely on her dream lover. She arched up, seeking to take him deeper into her body and dug her nails into the hard ridges of his sweaty, rippling shoulders.

"There! Right there. Yes!" she cried, as he drove hard into her core.

Endless heat churned through her belly, fierce tremors igniting between her wet thighs. She fought back the sudden urge to blush. She might not do this kind of thing with men she didn't know—or for that matter with men she did—but this was a dream, not real life. There was no reason for decorum in a dream. No reason to reflect on all those words about virtue and saving oneself for marriage that her parents had doled out time and again. And there sure as heck wasn't a reason to be Ms. Nice Girl, she realized with giddy clarity.

"I want you to make me come," she demanded, her embarrassment long forgotten. "I want you to grind your fist against my pussy and make me come so hard I scream."

Her dream lover pulled his magical mouth from her breast, tipped back his head and laughed a delightfully deep chuckle. For the first time she saw his eyes—a startling blue that churned with savage hunger. He was rugged as she'd first noticed, but he was also damned attractive. Just a little tidying—trim the hair, lose the beard—oh yeah, he'd be perfect. Exactly the type of man needed to set free her too long subdued wild side.

He did as she asked, eased his fingers out and rocked his fist hard against her throbbing pussy. His knuckles rubbed against her sensitized cleft, parting her labia and coaxing her distended clit with almost painful pleasure.

Anita's muscles tensed as the orgasm built inside her, her juices dampening the crotch of her panties and slacks. Then the dampness turned to an all out waterfall of sticky moisture, and she couldn't stop from writhing against him, grinding her slick vulva harder against his fist, screaming her ecstasy.

"Yes! Fuck me! Harder! Faster!" She gripped his big, muscled body tighter in her hands, driving her short nails into his honed flesh until she knew crescents would mar his glistening skin for days.

Her screams continued as the come drained from the quivering center of her pussy and soaked his hand. When he'd milked the last of her wetness he brought his hand to his nose and inhaled her musky arousal. He didn't need to get his fingers so close to his face, she could smell the tang of her sex on the air, alive in the forest-themed bedroom. A bedroom that looked shockingly, unnervingly familiar.

Her dream lover, who suddenly looked a lot more real than she cared to acknowledge, shook his head and cracked a smug grin. "Well hell, here I thought you looked like a nun, but I guess you really do deserve that dominatrix title after all." His grin edged higher, a mischievous twinkle lighting the need that burned in his eyes. "Except you aren't the one dishing out control here. Are you, princess?"

Anita's heart slammed wildly against her rib cage. She scuttled backward until she collided with the knotty pine headboard. The man who wasn't her dream lover at all, but a real life flesh-and-blood human being lost his grin and scowled at her.

In that instant, she knew this wasn't a time for propriety or to seek divine intervention, but to curse for all she was worth.

Holy shit! What the fuck had she just done?

# Chapter Two

ಐ

Zane stared at the red tinge streaking the woman's face and brightening the freckles on her upturned nose, and his gut tightened. Was she not who he thought she was? Why the hell did she look like he'd just taken her virginity on prom night and her daddy had found out the next day?

"What's the problem, princess?" he asked, crawling up the bed until he was almost on top of her—close enough to feel the warmth of her breath in his face, and to see the gold tints in her amber eyes as well as his own reflection.

He looked like shit. No wonder she'd freaked out the first time she'd gotten a good look at him. He edged back and came to his feet. "I don't usually look quite this rough. I got caught in the storm on my way back up from the lake."

Her passion-reddened lips turned down in a frown, and he felt his own scowl return. What the fuck was he doing? Apologizing for his appearance to a woman who'd been paid to entertain him? So far, she was the only one who'd been entertained.

He drew to his full height of six two and glared at her. "Look, I know you were paid to, ah, take care of me tonight, but touching my stuff isn't part of the deal."

Her frown died and she huffed. "Touching your stuff? Well, excuse me, Mr. Matthews, but what I did is called cleaning, something I don't think you've quite figured out yet."

Mr. Matthews? So, she knew who he was. Regardless of her soft and sweet schoolgirl looks, he obviously had the right woman—sex goddess—or whatever she wanted to be called. The blush had to have been a fluke, or maybe she was pissed off at him. He'd never been good at sensing when something was wrong with a woman. Trina's departure was proof enough of that.

Even if she was a pissed off sex goddess it didn't give her the right to cop an attitude with him, especially not when she was sitting on his bed with all her feminine assets exposed for his viewing pleasure. His attention drifted to her high, firm breasts, her large nipples, hard and bright pink from when he'd rolled them with his teeth. He journeyed down her flat stomach to her opened slacks. Her vibrant red and black panties were tugged low and a dash of curly, sable pubic hair trailed upward. Beneath that dark thatch was a pussy so tight, wet and hot, his body hummed with the need to bury his cock into it and fuck her all night long.

As if she'd picked up on his thoughts, she gasped and shot fast as a bullet beneath the bed covers. Ignoring the urgent throb of his shaft, he yanked his gaze back to her face. Her high cheekbones flared back to that bright crimson shade. She looked as frightened as a cornered church mouse, and nothing like a dominatrix.

"Stop that!" she screeched, gripping the covers tight against her collarbone.

Zane didn't bother to hold back his chuckle. Between her low cut panties—so loud and gauzy they practically begged to be removed with his teeth—and her back and forth flashes from good girl to she-devil, the woman was just too damned amusing and contradictory not to laugh over. "Don't tell me that bothers you, princess. A dominatrix who blushes from a mere look? Why don't I believe that?"

She pulled the covers higher yet, until they blanketed her long, creamy neck. She could hide herself all she wanted. He already knew just how tantalizing her delicate curves were. More, he knew just how sweet they tasted. Most of them anyway. The rest he'd get his mouth on soon. Right after he relieved her of those vibrant panties, he'd dip his tongue into her creamy center and have a nice, long lick followed by a nice, long suck, followed by an even nicer, even longer fuck.

His cock jumped, rubbing impatiently at his boxers and he bit back a curse. That his penis was hard enough to explode at the slightest touch proved just how overdue he was for an afternoon of carnal bliss.

"I—I'm not..." she sputtered.

Nun. The idea swept through his mind a second time as her eyes flared wide. Wasn't that just the way his life went? Here he was ready to come in his jeans and the woman responsible looked as eager as a hooker in a room full of eunuchs. She'd been excited enough for both of them moments ago. Surely he could get her that way again with only the slightest provocation.

He took a step forward and flashed a hungry grin. "You're not what?"

"I'm not supposed to get naked!"

His mouth fell flat at her unexpected announcement.

That was her beef? It was okay for him to drop his drawers and let her have a whack or fifty at him so long as she stayed clothed? But, no. That couldn't be the reason for her behavior. Not after seeing how much she'd enjoyed being undressed five minutes ago, after hearing her impassioned cries to fuck her harder. Which meant she must be pissed off. Not at him as he'd first guessed, but at herself for stepping outside the norm. There was some small measure of comfort in knowing this wasn't her typical routine. Still, what the hell was the point of hiring someone to dominate you, if the someone in question wasn't going to get naked and join in the festivities?

"Whose rules?" Zane asked, broadening his stance.

"What?"

"Whose rule is that, because if you ask me it's pretty fucking stupid."

Her eyes edged wider for just an instant, then narrowed. "Mr. Matthews, I did not come here to be—"

"I'd say we know each other well enough for you to call me Zane. And if you didn't come here to have your mouse clicked, then what the hell are you here for?"

"To have my mouse clicked," she mouthed, the color leaving her face in a rush and making her look all of sixteen. "Oh my gracious! This is not what you…"

He crossed his arms over his chest and raised an eyebrow. "Yeah?"

"I…I…I have to go to the bathroom."

\* \* \* \* \*

"Heavens above, what an idiot." Anita chastised her reflection in the small mirror that hung over the bathroom sink.

Her lips were swollen and red, her eyes bleary and her short, mousy-brown curls tousled to distraction. She looked like she'd just undergone a thorough session of lovemaking. Maybe because she had to a lesser extent. How could she have let that brute paw her that way? He looked like Mountain Man Jack for goodness sake. And the way she'd begged him to make her climax. Oh, if her parents could see her now they'd probably cast her out as a fallen angel. Well, if nothing else her actions had certainly disproved Jordan's belief that good girl Anita could never be naughty.

*Jordan!* She'd forgotten all about her friend.

She told her she'd call as soon as she left Mr. Matthews— Zane's cabin. What time was it? Was it even Friday? What the heck was she thinking falling asleep on a stranger's bed? Probably the same thing she'd been thinking when she'd felt that same stranger's sensuous mouth foraging on her nipples. His long, strong fingers spreading her feminine lips and caressing her to the pinnacle of a raging orgasm.

Moisture seeped between her thighs and her sex thrummed with the urge to be fondled by those deft hands all over again. With an inward groan, she shook the thought away. Quite clearly she hadn't been thinking when she'd fallen asleep any more than she was now. At least not with more than a few brain cells. All day long she'd been agreeing to things she knew better than to accept. It had to be lack of sleep. The past week the insomnia she'd battled the better part of her life had grown increasingly worse. As a result, she'd spent too much time cleaning her house, arranging her bookcase, and numerous other meaningless pursuits in the middle of the night. Yes, that was it. Lack of sleep had finally gotten to her, made her delirious, made her do things she wouldn't normally do.

"Princess?"

"Anita." She slapped a hand over her mouth at the automatic response. She wasn't supposed to tell him that!

"Mistress Anita, or just Anita?"

Mistress Anita! Great, he was convinced she was a dominatrix. How did she explain this was all one huge mistake? That she was about as far from a dominatrix as a girl could get? If only Jordan had given her a little advice on how to break the news to him. But no, all she'd said was 'If you aren't up to telling him I can't make it, you can always be my stand in.'

Her friend's high-pitched squeal of laughter pierced once more through Anita's mind. She squeezed her eyes tight to block it out. Jordan had no right laughing at her like that. So she didn't get off on spanking men or jamming her heel up their rear, or for that matter get off much at all regardless of the circumstances. She was still as sexual as the next girl, still had her fair share of fantasies she craved to explore. It all came down to the matter of finding the right ma—

"Anita?" Zane's deep baritone sounded through the bathroom door again. "Is something the matter? Or do you think you can open the door so I can use the john?"

She snorted at his choice of words. Lovely, she'd gotten off at the hands of Mr. Manners himself. Manners or not, the point couldn't be argued he'd pleased her and then some, made her forget herself long enough to let loose and be a little naughty.

He wasn't the right man to let lose with. Not even close to the one she'd imagined exploring her secret desires with. But what if that man didn't exist? What if she spent her whole life looking and never found him? She wouldn't shrivel up and die if he never came along, but she also might not ever know what letting her inhibitions go and following instinct felt like. She'd never know what it felt like to be bad.

She could do this. Not go all out and continue on the sexual journey they'd begun, but she could do the job Zane believed she had come here to do. She'd always wondered how Jordan felt being the controller and this was the perfect opportunity to learn. Out here in the middle of nowhere, no one would ever have to know she succumbed to temptation. No one would judge her actions. At least, no one she couldn't placate with a lengthy confession and several dozen Hail Marys.

"You can do this," Anita assured herself. "It will be fun. He wants you to do this," she added in way of encouragement.

And really, she knew how. At least, she had a good idea the kind of punishment Zane expected thanks to Jordan's many shared exploits. All she had to do was muster up the courage to put her secondhand knowledge to use.

As far as what she had to work with…

It would help if she had the appropriate apparel for the job. Since she didn't and Zane had already seen her body anyway, she would just have to make do with what God gave her. Allowing the sheet to drop to the floor, she studied her reflection in the mirror, scrutinizing her small curves in a way she'd never before dared. Her breasts might not be that big, but they were high and firm. Her nipples were larger than she'd have liked, but surely something like that wouldn't turn a man off.

She traced her fingers over a dusky bud, recalling the way Zane had drawn it into his mouth and made her so unbearably hot and needy. Moistness gathered at the junction of her thighs, and her nipples grew swollen with the memory. The fleeting idea that to touch herself so intimately was immoral skipped through her mind. She shook it away to concentrate on her body—upbringing had no place in this cabin tonight. Neither did propriety. She had to be the woman she was in her dreams. The wild one who said and did exactly what was on her mind.

Forcing that daring part of herself to the forefront, Anita did another, more meticulous perusal, noting each flaw and asset in turn. Maybe she didn't have an hourglass figure, or even a pretty face. But she was cute and trim, and clearly to a guy like Zane Matthews that was enough. It certainly had been enough for him to strip her half naked and bury his fingers deep inside her.

She shivered at the memory, fingering her nipple-hardened breasts as this time she let it develop in full detail. The way he'd parted her aching pussy and pierced deep into her core had been more primal than anything she'd ever experienced. His big, rough and sinful fingers had kneaded against her throbbing sex, petting her distended clitoris until the storm that still blistered through the cabin walls was little more than a whisper on the wind. She burned to let him do that again, to allow those clever fingers to plunge into her pussy once more. To feel the sensuous mouth and powerful tongue that had feasted upon her nipples suckling at her cleft and slicing into her center.

She trembled as her blood heated, her heart beating wildly against her rib cage. She rubbed her palm against her mound, wishing the slacks and panties would disappear. She ached to touch herself, to end this burning—

"I'm coming in," Zane barked, shaking her from her hedonistic daze.

She'd no sooner lifted her hands from her body then the door pushed open. The man of the hour stood just outside the frame, his torso wonderfully stripped and glistening in a way that made her fingers itch to touch. Her blood pulsed with the anticipation of doing just that and she took a step toward him.

Smiling in a way she hoped looked as naughty as it felt, Anita gave him a thorough once over, taking him in as she had never allowed herself her to do to a man before, all the while fighting a blush that she refused to let free. That his body was magnificent with its streamlined angles and finely honed muscles was a given. And his face—once you got past the beard and hair in need of a trim, it looked darned good. Damned good—naughty girls didn't say darned. And she *was* naughty. Naughty Mistress Nita.

At least for the next few hours.

* * * * *

Zane wasn't sure what to think about the heat that had suddenly overtaken Anita's expression. She'd gone from uncertain to looking like she wanted to attack him in the space of a heartbeat. She'd also lost the sheet and her large, rigid nipples were pointing right at him. Almost as if to say 'go ahead, big guy, have a suck'.

"Use the bathroom, then we have work to do." Her high breasts jiggling and her slacks slowly making their way down her hips, she brushed past him. She turned back at the last second, winked, and smacked his ass hard.

He bit back a wince. Apparently, Anita had gotten past her little overstep of getting naked in front of him and was now in full domination mode. Well, he had news for her. He wasn't going to be Mr. Submissive no matter what kind of charm she laid on the line. She wanted to smack his ass in the heat of the moment that was one thing, but no way in hell was she going to tie him down and paddle away.

Ten minutes later, Zane sat with his back against the big bed's knotty pine headboard and his hands secured with a bungee cord behind him. Why the fuck he thought she'd back down was beyond him. He'd seen the anticipation come into her eyes the moment she'd located the cord. For some reason he still thought she'd back down, turn three shades of red, and kindly excuse herself to the bathroom. He'd been wrong, and now he was shackled to the fucking bed, and she'd found one of his three-sided drafting rulers and was whacking it against her palm.

She stilled with the tip of the ruler in her hand, her eyes dancing with excitement and her naked breasts jostling with every move she made. "You've been a bad boy, Zane. Tell

Naughty Mistress Nita what you've done and I'll make it all better."

*What he'd done?* He'd decided to give into a night of free and possibly kinky sex. Just not *this* kinky. "Look, Anita, this really isn't—"

She whacked the ruler against her palm, flinching as it struck her soft flesh, turning it deep red. "Naughty Mistress Nita! Get it right—" Her mouth curved in an devilish smile "—or do you want me to punish you?"

Zane's cock throbbed with the smack of the ruler against her palm and the insidious tilt of her lips. She smacked the ruler again and all the blood in his body shot directly to his groin while his balls drew mercilessly tight in his suddenly too snug jeans. He really wasn't getting turned on by this. Really, he wasn't. At least, not that much.

"How would you punish me?" he asked against his own better judgment.

She paused with the ruler secured in her fist and her forehead knitted. Between the thin lines creasing her brow and the freckles streaked vividly across her pert little nose she looked thoughtful and sweet, and way too damned young for either of their goods.

Shit, he should've thought a little harder before deciding to make use of her presence. Or maybe he just should have thought with his brain instead of his dick. The guys said she was certified, but that didn't necessarily mean she was. What if she wasn't a seasoned dominatrix at all, but a minor out to make a few dollars?

"What do you like, Zane?"

Anita's low, throaty voice cut into his thoughts. He focused on her hand as she fondled his ruler with long, purposeful strokes. What he wouldn't do to feel that small capable hand wrapped around his cock, fondling him with those same sure, steady strokes. He lifted his gaze to her breasts and deduced she wouldn't even have to relinquish her grip on the ruler. He could just as happily bury his shaft between those pale, smooth globes and pump against their weight until he came all over her chest. He gazed even higher and grinned. Or maybe he'd skip her breasts and go right for the honey hole. Those rosy red lips would make the perfect fit for—

"Do you have any fetishes or do you want to share mine?"

Zane's thoughts came to a crashing halt as he met her lust-filled gaze. He swallowed hard with the realization of just how far she'd taken him with little more than a few idle strokes of a ruler. She might look like a minor, but she didn't act like one, not with those practiced moves. Sure as hell not with those eyes.

"You have a fetish?" he questioned, amazed how damned badly he wanted to hear about it. Maybe her schoolgirl image was why she was so good at her job. More men than him had to get turned on by her cutesy cum naughty routine.

"Yes, I do," she purred, rubbing her thumb over the tip of the ruler as she wet her lips, "and you're going to make Naughty Mistress Nita very happy."

# Chapter Three

Zane waited half-afraid, half-excited, but mostly hard as hell as Anita rocked back on the bed, pulling her feet from beneath her. She removed her socks and rolled them into a neat little ball before depositing them on the floor, then leaned back on her hands. Slowly, she straightened her legs, extending her right foot to the inside of his widespread thighs. He drew in a sharp breath when her toes pressed against his engorged cock through his jeans.

Arousal darkened her eyes and further peaked her nipples. "Mmm...you like being tied up, don't you, Zane?"

He never would have thought so before this but hell, maybe he did. He shifted on the bed and her kneading toes nipped into the solid length of his cock with a pleasure so divine it was on the edge of painful. The kind of painful that had a groan slipping from his mouth. He liked being tied up, he realized in that moment. He liked it a whole hell of a lot when Anita was involved. "You do good work."

She hesitated an instant, an unidentifiable emotion passing through her eyes, then continued her ministrations. "If you like that, then you're really going to like this."

Anita lifted her soft sole to his bare chest and curled her short toenails against the muscle, biting sinfully and oh-so-erotically into his flesh. She flashed a brazen smile as she lifted her foot higher yet, then paused with it just in front of his mouth.

"Open up, Zane," she said huskily. "Lick my toes, suck them until they're dripping wet and then kiss them dry."

He'd liked to suck on her salty, sweet center until it was dripping wet, then kiss it dry instead. Only that didn't appear to be an option—not yet anyway. For now he'd play his part and suck on her toes, but when she was finished toying with him it would be payback time. And the last thing he wanted her to suck on was his toe.

Concentrating on the hedonistic sight of her exposed, firm breasts, Zane opened his mouth. She slipped her big toe between his lips and rolled the underside of it along the lower one. He laved his tongue across the end, and she jerked away with a peal of girlish laughter.

He gaped at her, struck by her reaction. Was this all part of her schoolgirl act? And if so, was her giggling really supposed to turn him on? Okay, judging by the way his cock responded, with a restless thumping against his zipper, her act was working, in a really twisted sort of way.

"Are you laughing?" he asked.

She rolled back on the bed, her giggles undulating in turn with her breasts, bringing Zane's own amusement to the surface. "I can't help it, that tickles!"

His amusement faded and he frowned. It tickled? Schoolgirl act or not, he couldn't see a practiced dominatrix admitting to something like that. But then he'd already determined she wasn't an uneducated minor either. Maybe she was still in training, or just given the red flag to work the field solo. That might explain how she could blush and appear knowledgeable at the same time.

"Do you always laugh when men suck your toes?" he inquired.

"Men don't normally..." Anita's laughter died instantly. She straightened and reclaimed her hold on the ruler. "I mean, no. Of course not." She levered her foot back to his mouth and rested her toes against the seam. Her shameless smile back in place, she fingered the measuring stick. "Keep licking, or face Naughty Nita's ruler."

No. He didn't think so. Something told him she wouldn't really use it on him. But then he'd been wrong about the whole bungee cord thing. Still, he had to tempt fate. He'd never had the opportunity to experiment with anything beyond vanilla sex in his short-lived and pathetic excuse for a marriage. He'd be a sorry excuse for a red-blooded man to let a moment like this one pass him by. After all if Anita was as new to this game as he thought, she was liable to go along with just about anything he wanted. With a little encouragement she was, anyway.

"What if I want to lick something else?" Zane asked huskily. He lifted his own foot to rub against the slacks that covered her parted thighs. She sucked in a loud breath when he reached her open zipper and stroked his big toe against her damp panties.

The foot she'd placed to his mouth fell back to the comforter, and her eyes flickered wide on a moan. "Like what?"

He smirked at how easily she turned on. Trina never so much as gasped when he touched her, let alone considered allowing him to stick his toe into her center. Hell, she'd barely wanted his penis there. "Like Naughty Nita's pussy."

Her eyes edged wider. He drove his toe against the vibrant material, burying it into her damp slit as far as the thin material allowed. She moaned again, but made no attempt to move outside of the instinctive bucks of her juicy sex against his foot.

"Oh. That isn't possible," she said lazily. Her lids fell slowly over her eyes as he felt the tension leak from her body. "I'm here to command you, to fulfill your needs."

"I *need* to lick your pussy."

Anita's eyes drifted further closed and she whimpered in the way she had done earlier, when he'd first removed her bra and found the delicious treasures beneath. Her soft, little mewls had his cock rock solid and ready to explode then. Now, he was hard as granite and yearning to break free of his bonds. Of course, he could get out of the bungee cord bindings if he really wanted, but it would be much more fun to make her do the work, to watch her pet the tight, wet folds of her labia the way he burned to do.

"You like that, don't you, princess, feeling my toe fucking you? If you move your panties to the side, I can take it even deeper. We can pretend it's my tongue. That I'm licking your pussy the way I *need* to do."

Her eyes flew wide, revealing passion-riddled amber and gold. She bucked up one last time, showering the air with the heady essence of her sex, and removed herself from his reach.

"Your other needs," she said firmly.

A blush stole over her cheeks as she righted her slacks and did up the zipper. She glanced at her nipple-hardened breasts, and the color streamed higher.

Had she only just remembered that she was stripped to the waist, or what the hell was up with the reemergence of her blush?

Zane narrowed his eyes at her, and she jerked her attention away. She darted her gaze around the bedroom, finally stopping by the doorway. She nodded in the direction of the fishing pole he'd tossed down when he'd entered the cabin to find her asleep on his bed. "How about we roll you over and I whip that pole across your ass a few times? Or I could get my dress shoes out of the car and kick you."

He smirked at her words. So she was backpedaling, was she? *It's a little too late for that, princess.* She had him primed and ready. Between the smell of her heated sex and her drenched panties he knew she was just as eager to play. "That sounds like fun, really, but I still want to lick your pussy."

Anita looked back at him, her cheeks burning with vivid color and her freckles so dark they looked like they'd been drawn on, and shook her finger. "Zane!"

He bit back his snicker at the way her shaking finger fit her schoolgirl, or maybe her nun routine to a tee. "Do you like to be eaten out, Nita? Does it make you hot, horny and heavy inside? Or do you like to watch? Do you get off on slapping men? Beating them up and making them scream with pain? Does that really do it for you?"

She pressed her unpainted lips together, balled her hands into fists, and shook her head. Her chaotic hair bounced righteously around her face. Her eyes flamed with emotion. She was either going to explode or cry, he wasn't quite certain.

Not much to Zane's surprise, given he couldn't read women worth a damn, she didn't do either, simply stuck her finger back out and wagged it at him. "If you want punishment, Zane Matthews, I suggest you start talking, otherwise I have another appointment."

"Two in one night?" He raised an eyebrow. Shitty at reading women or not, he was finding it increasingly difficult to believe she was a dominatrix of any kind. Even one new to the job had to be more convincing than she was at this moment. "You do get around, don't you, Naughty Mistress Nita," he added on a mocking smile.

"One tonight," she bit out, stumbling off the bed and to her feet. She snatched her sweater and bra from the floor and swiveled on her heel. "You just lost your chance."

\* \* \* \* \*

In the safety of the bathroom, Anita slipped on her bra and tugged her sweater over her beyond-help hair. Good Lord Almighty, she needed to get far away from the panty-wetting brute in the other room. She thought she could handle controlling him, thought she could dominate him without wanting more.

She'd been wrong!

She wanted more, wanted more so badly her pussy throbbed with raw ache. Why a guy like him, rugged and gruff as could be, could light her typically sensible fire so easily, she had no idea. He wasn't close to the man she planned to share her fantasies with, but the idea of him flicking his rough tongue over her clit…all he had to do was mention it and she was ready to beg for him to put his words into action.

And that isn't what she came here for!

She hadn't come here to dominate him either, though for a short while she'd managed to convince herself it was a good idea. She'd simply come to break an appointment. And she would. Playtime was over. She had her visit to naughty land, now it was time to face facts — she was a minister's daughter, not a red, hot, and willing vixen — and get home to her big, empty house, and spend yet another long, sleepless night picking at imaginary dust bunnies.

Doing her best to force thoughts of strong, male tongues in pink, puffy zones from her mind, Anita finger-combed her hair, then retraced her steps from the minuscule bathroom to the bedroom. It was time to go. Before desire won over better judgment.

"I'm sorry you didn't get your money's worth, but — "

"But, princess, the night's still young." Zane's powerful arm came out of nowhere, clamping around her middle and pulling her tight against a solid wall she quickly recognized as his chest. "I'm sure we'll both be more than satisfied before it's over."

"Zane — "

He covered her mouth with his free hand and dropped his lips to her ear, his coarse beard scrapping erotically against her sensitive flesh. He whispered hoarsely, "Are you going to scream? Are you scared? What's going through your mind, Naughty Mistress Nita? Tell me you don't want to lie back on that bed and let me suck on your pussy."

The hand at her waist moved beneath the hem of her sweater and slid upward, beneath the underwire of her bra. He cupped her taut breast in his big, rough palm and she bit back a moan of raw hunger. He stroked her nipple and she gasped as it drew tight, rippling endless fire deep within her and making her limbs tremble. Wetness pooled heavily between her thighs and she clenched them together.

"This isn't how it's supposed to work!" she cried out.

He unhooked her bra, allowing it to fall discarded at their feet, then worked her other nipple, twisting and turning, plucking the stiff bud between his fingers. Her breathing grew harsh and erratic. His nearly as loud and uneven.

"Maybe not, but you do want it, don't you?" he rasped fiercely. "Tell me the truth."

"No!" she lied, though the urge to give in flamed through her, hammering as hot as the blood that careened through her veins.

"Right. And this doesn't excite you." Zane ground his thick, erect shaft against her back, and palmed her breast in his hand, squeezing roughly. "The feel of my callused fingers gripping your breasts. My hot breath in your ear. My cock pressed up against your back. I bet it's making your panties wet, isn't it, Anita?"

"No. Yes. Zane," she wailed, fighting the urge to squirm, to press back against his rock solid arousal and impale herself from behind. She wanted to sink onto his cock and explode with passion. To let him show her everything she'd been missing out on in life, to allow him to share in every one of her most secret fantasies.

Oh, Lord, how had things gotten so out of control?

She was supposed to walk out of the bathroom, get into her car, and drive away nearly the same good girl she'd been when she arrived. That's not what was happening—not even close. What was happening didn't even fall into the dominatrix boundaries. At least, not as she understood them.

"You aren't supposed to touch me," she said, registering the husk in her tone. "You keep doing it, and it isn't how's it supposed to work. Jordan doesn't allow—"

"Jordan?" His movements stilled and she heard the anger reverberate in his words. "Is that your boyfriend? Is that why you're acting so upset about this?"

"*She's* my...my instructor. She says we shouldn't let the men touch us this way. That's not what we're here for."

Anita could almost hear his smile as his fingers returned to their quest of slowly driving her out of her mind, which incidentally was working perfectly. "Do you want me to stop? Do you want me to behave like all those other men and lie still while you beat the shit out of me?"

It was so wrong of her to want him. Someone she typically would never even consider dating, let alone sharing her body with. Someone her parents would never approve of. It wasn't like her at all. Yet she wanted him so badly it hurt.

Muttering an apology to above for her wayward behavior, she moaned her answer. She sank back against the sturdy length of his thick cock, giving in to all he had to offer and the long unfulfilled appetite that burned uncontrollably now, aching to be set free.

"I didn't think so," Zane growled, nipping a wet kiss below her ear. "I bet you get tired of always being the one in control, don't you, Anita? Pushing all those men around, spanking them, kicking them, doing everything they beg for and more. I bet sometimes you want to be the one spanked, the one begging for punishment."

His wicked words spoke to the daring part of her that had lain dormant for way too long. A part that craved everything he said. A part she'd been raised to deny. She couldn't deny it any longer, wouldn't. Not when the idea of being completely and utterly out of control, of being dominated at Zane's strong hands had her entire body trembling and her pussy drenched with the juices of arousal.

She nodded her assent, and he pinched her breast cruelly, yet in a way that fired every sexual neuron she possessed. "Not good enough. Tell me, princess. I need to hear the words. What do you want me to do to you?"

So much, so very many things that she didn't know where to begin, or if she could even speak aloud what she'd only fantasized about.

Anita picked an item from his list, hoping he'd want to indulge every bit as much as she. "I want you to spank me," she whispered, feeling the blush creep into her cheeks.

"I can't hear you when you whisper. Say it like you mean it."

She drew in a ragged breath, then blurted loud and clear, "I want to be spanked. I want to be punished. Dominate me, Zane!"

"Why, Anita? What did you do? Were you a bad girl?"

She gulped at the way he continued to goad her. "Y—yes. I was naughty. Very naughty. I…" *Pretended to be someone I wasn't and just look where it got me.*

Not that she was sorry. Maybe tomorrow or the next day, but not now. Not when she was so very close to once again coming undone in the arms of a man who was more than capable of showing her the kind of pleasure she'd always secretly craved.

"How should I punish you?" he asked, twisting her nipple hard between his fingers. He moved his other hand down her belly and unbuttoned her slacks, coaxing the soft down beneath her panties with a single coarse finger. "Should I torment you with my hands, or something else?"

"What else?" she squeaked out, struggling for coherent thought as his finger edged ever closer to her pulsating vulva, to the heat that coiled endlessly in need of release.

"What do you want?" he questioned, the growl in his voice further churning her insides. "You wanted to use that fishing pole on me. I could tell how excited you were by the idea. Is that what you want me to do to you? Swat that long rod against your ass? Or how about an oar? Should I paddle your pretty little behind with an oar?"

"I—I don't know. I've never…try. Just try. Command me, Zane," she begged shamelessly, as his finger entered her and rubbed over her raw nub. "Anything you want. Anything at all. I'm yours."

# Chapter Four

ℬ

Zane stared down at the plump white ass splayed out on his lap and licked his lips with anticipation. He really didn't want to paddle Anita. At least, not with an oar, or even a fishing pole. With his hands, that was another story. Trina had never allowed him to look at her like this, with her lush body laid across his lap and her tight, wet, glistening pink pussy exposed for his perusal. But Anita wasn't Trina, just like he couldn't believe she was a dominatrix.

Sex goddess...that he could see. She certainly had him ready to beg to bury his engorged cock deep into her center and fuck her senseless.

Only he didn't have to beg. She'd already offered herself to him.

He started to reach for the pole he'd rested against the bed beside him, but then drew back. There was no rush. The rain still fell in heavy sheets outside and, besides, darkness had set in. He had nowhere to go tonight. Nowhere beyond his wildest fantasies with a woman he couldn't get a handle on to save his life.

Maybe not a handle, but certainly his hands. He stroked his finger down the crack of her smooth ass, enjoying the way her cheeks puckered at his touch. He dragged his finger back up the seam, burying it between her firm buttocks as he went. She drew in a shallow breath, and he grinned at the lust thick in her gasp.

"If you like that, princess, you're really going to like it when it's my tongue sliding into all your milky white crevices."

She wriggled on his lap, so that her slacks slid even father down her long, toned legs. Her pussy gyrated against his jeans, dampening the material over his swollen cock as she brought her hands to his thighs. "Please…"

"Please what?" he asked, his balls drawing tight as her fingernails bit hard into his muscled flesh. "Do you want me to spank you now?"

She panted breathlessly, writhing uncontrollably. "Yes!"

Zane took one more swipe of her round, silky ass, then palmed the fishing pole he'd stripped of its tackle moments before. He swallowed hard as he raised the rod in the air. Now that they were actually doing this, he wasn't so sure he could go through with it. He wouldn't hurt her. She'd admittedly never done this kind of thing before. At least had someone do it to her, and he was all but convinced the opposite was true too.

"Zane?" she questioned impatiently.

Damn. She wanted it. He had to do it. For her. "It's coming, princess. Ready?"

She nodded, her soft sable curls swishing enticingly along her newly bared nape. He drew a steadying breath and brought the pole down with a gentle whack.

"I can't feel it," she mumbled.

He grunted. Shit. He couldn't do this. Maybe Trina had been right for him after all. No, she hadn't. Anita was the kind of woman he needed. Fearless. Willing to try anything. A sexual adventurer with the prowess to match.

He raised the rod again and brought it down a bit more soundly. A thin red line colored her supple, creamy flesh, and his cock throbbed with wild excitement, even as his gut twisted with guilt. "How about that? Did you feel that?"

Her nails pinched deeper into his thigh, bringing a guttural groan into his parched throat. "Oh, yes! I can feel it."

"Do you like it?"

"I like you," she answered throatily, "I like knowing you're doing it to me."

It wasn't the answer he'd expected. It was far and above better than a simple 'yes'. Setting the pole aside, he palmed her ass, squeezed the tender cheeks, then spanked her hard with his hand, the way she had wanted. She responded with a throaty whimper. He responded with a thundering rush of power and emotion. He spanked her once more and his cock jumped, demanding to be set free. "Do you want me to keep going, or do you want something else? Do you want me to tongue your pussy now?"

She paused for an instant, then uttered a quiet, "Yes."

More than eager to finally get his mouth on the sensitive lips of her pussy and the even more sensitive nub hidden beneath them, Zane turned Anita in his lap. Her slacks and panties pooled at her ankles and her wet, slick sex shone through its damp, curly covering as brilliantly as her eyes shone against the backdrop of her flushed face. Her freckles stood out vividly on the tip of her upturned nose, but she didn't look cute any longer. She looked hot and sexy as hell. And completely and utterly his for the taking.

He caught an erect nipple between his thumb and forefinger and tugged. She squeaked out a gasp, her wide amber eyes contracting in response, and his need to command rekindled to a fever pitch.

"And when I finish," he asked hoarsely, gliding his rough palm down her belly and through her pubic hair to skim against her damp mound, "will you do the same for me? Will you take my cock in your mouth and suck on it until you swallow my come?"

"Yes," she panted, as he strummed a single finger along the fringes of her distended, quivering clitoris. "I want to taste every inch of you."

"Why?" he demanded, applying just a bit more pressure.

She tilted her hips, instinctively trying to bring him closer. "Because."

"Because why?" he pressed, coaxing her with one hard stroke.

She shuddered at his touch, moaning, "Because you excite me."

Zane's finger stilled, as did his irregular breathing. "I do?"

"Yes. No one's ever..." Color flirted in her cheeks and she trailed off.

"Say it, don't hold back. Tell me." God, he had to know, had to hear that he still knew how to make a woman feel good. He'd told himself he could, believed he could, but right up until this moment he hadn't been certain, nor had he realized how deeply Trina's deceit had bothered him. Anita could make things right again, make him believe in his abilities. All she had to do was say 'yes' one more time.

She closed her eyes and responded in a low husky tone. "You excite me so much, Zane. No one's ever made me feel this way before, made me want to let go so completely. I'm so hot and wet. I feel like I could float, and at the same time I'm so tense, so tight, like I'm going to burst. You do that to me, you make me want to explode with just your words."

He swallowed hard at the emotion that clogged his throat. Still, for his own selfish reasons he needed more. Maybe while he was at it, he could get to the bottom of her endless contradictions. "You're a dominatrix, Anita. All those men you work with, not one of them makes you hot and wet? Not a single one makes you want to explode?"

"I don't do..." She opened her eyes and shook her head. "No. Not like this."

He grinned complacently. He might not be any closer to uncovering the truth about her, but he felt like the weight of the world had been lifted from his shoulders. In a way, it had. At least the weight that rested on them these past few months. He didn't think twice about his next move, but bent and took her mouth with his.

On a shallow intake of breath her soft, unpainted lips yielded, and he swept his tongue inside, relishing her sweetness and warmth. He feasted on her flavor, on her flowery scent and the gift she'd unknowingly given him. All the while the fire that flamed inside him burnt higher, energizing for a release to shake the very mountain the cabin rested upon.

One velvety swipe of his tongue against her seeking one and he pulled back. "I'd say I'm a pretty damned lucky man."

Anita looked at him for several long moments without saying a word, then asked softly yet brazenly, in a way that fit her character perfectly, "You taste so good, but what happened to licking me?"

Zane's grin edged wider. He hadn't forgotten about that. Not by a long shot. But it was all the more reassuring to know she still wanted it as badly as he did. He set her back on the bed and tugged off her slacks and panties. He deposited the clothing on the floor, then stood back to indulge in the sight of her small, firm curves.

Her weight braced on her elbows, she gaped at him. "What are you doing?"

"Lie back," he ordered gruffly. "And spread your legs."

Red rushed up her neck and tinged her chest as her eyes drew wider. "But—"

"No, buts. Just do it."

Slowly, she parted her legs, until her shimmering pink pussy peeked from between her shuddering thighs. His fingers itched to grab hold of her knees and spread her legs wide enough to accommodate his broad shoulders, to latch his mouth onto her glistening bud. Only it was much more exciting to make her do it herself, to see the color that flamed in her face and over her chest. She might not have as much prowess as he gave her credit for, but she would before they were done here tonight.

"Good. But not far enough. I want them wide open and your knees bent."

She lifted her head and gave it a shake. "Zane, I can't do—"

"Do it, Naughty Mistress Nita! Live up to your name."

With a barely audible squeak, Anita rested her head back and spread her thighs wider. Even wider than what he'd imagined she'd do without further encouragement. Zane's penis pushed hard against his zipper and the blood, which had been alternating between his brain and his balls since the moment she'd shown up on his bed, finally made up its mind his balls were indeed the better of the two options.

"Hmmm... Nice. Very nice," he growled. "Do you know what I see?"

"N-no."

"A wet, hot pussy trembling for my tongue."

"Oh, Lord," she groaned.

He moved to the side of the bed so he could see her face and she could see his actions as well. Her nose was scrunched up and her cheeks burning with vivid color. Her lips mouthed nearly soundless words. He could only make out one or two, and those were unfathomable in that they sounded like she was praying. He shook the far-fetched notion away to concentrate completely on the flush that stained her face.

"Are you blushing, Anita? I've already seen all of you, how can you act so shy now? Is it me staring at your hot little pussy that bothers you? What will you do when I lick it, when I tongue your slippery lips and make you come in my mouth?"

Her lips stilled and she looked at him with wary eyes. "Zane..."

"What? What do you want, princess?" Refusing to be deterred by the caution in her gaze, he slid his hand to the burning bulge in his jeans and rubbed his erection through the confining material. Her breathing grew heavier as she watched, her breasts rising and falling in a climatic tempo until her wariness was replaced with pure animalistic need. Aware he had her complete attention, Zane yanked down the zipper, and pulled his rock hard cock through the slit in his boxers.

Anita's pupils contracted and her throat worked visibly as he took his engorged penis into his hand and stroked. Moisture beaded on the smooth, deep purple head and he rubbed his thumb over it in slow circles. "You look hungry, Anita. Hungry and impatient. Does watching me stroke my cock make you eager for my touch? For the feel of my mouth sucking at your salty, sweet clit?"

"Oh, yes! That's it," she panted, all but breathless, writhing on the bed. "I want you, Zane. I want you between my legs. I want your tongue on me!"

"Touch yourself," he commanded.

Her writhing stopped and she looked to him, the wariness he detected moments before back in full force. *"What?"*

Zane increased his grip on his cock and brought his hand up and down its rigid length with sure, steady strokes. She might look cautious, maybe even slightly nervous, but the sweat that glistened on her brow and her uneven breathing assured she was also excited. She'd told him she wanted this. Clearly, she just needed a push in the right direction. Someone to tell her it was okay to step outside the boundaries.

"I can tell how much you like watching me masturbate, princess. Now I want to watch you. Wet your fingers with your pussy juice and fondle your nipples."

She bit her lip and shook her head. "I…I can't."

"Yes. You can. And you will." He grinned smugly, as he turned her devices back on her. "Or do I have to get out the oar and paddle Naughty Mistress Nita?"

The slightest of squeaks escaped her mouth, and her sex flared. He knew he had her. "Do it, Anita. Touch yourself. Finger your pussy. Make yourself come."

"Ye—yes," she managed, as the pulse visible at her throat flitted to new heights.

Gradually, she slid her hand down her tight, pale body, between her widespread thighs, and skimmed the edge of her swollen vagina. She arched at the subtle touch, then wrenched her fingers back to the edge of her downy soft pubic hair.

"Good girl," Zane said hoarsely, his tension mounting with her torturously slow movements. "Now the rest of the way. Bury them inside."

"Zane—"

"Do it!"

Her breath coming in fits and starts, Anita feathered her fingers through her dark curls and petted her swollen cleft. Her eyes slowly closed and she released a soft, mewling cry. His cock throbbed in his palm with the sound, threatening to burst free and release come across the forest-themed comforter and all over her smooth, silky flesh. She moved her fingers faster, dipping deeper, eliciting loud, wet sucking sounds as her caution turned to mindless pleasure.

Liberated of whatever had troubled her, Anita brought her free hand to her breasts, tugging and twisting at each erect nipple in turn. Her body shuddered on the bed, her legs spreading wide, then clamping tightly together with her delirium. A keening moan of ecstasy drifted from her lips, building the already massive pressure at Zane's groin. She was so close to taking herself over the edge. All by her own hand. Without him.

Godammit, she wasn't going alone!

"That's enough," he barked, releasing his aching cock to strip the remainder of his clothes away. "I don't want you coming yet. I want my tongue inside you first."

# Chapter Five

෨

Anita was aware of the furious heat in her cheeks as Zane's wide shoulders pushed her thighs ever farther apart, but from the moment his rough tongue rasped over her clit she knew the warmth wasn't embarrassment but need. Lord, she needed him, in a way she couldn't even begin to explain.

She sought out his thick hair as his coarse beard abraded her tender flesh and his tongue flicked repeatedly between the folds of her soaking pussy. His movements became more forceful, and she bucked up wildly against his mouth, teetering on the edge of orgasm. Obviously her fervent prayers she'd make it through his demands without breaking down and confessing the truth had paid off, because the raw energy surging through her now beat anything she'd ever known. It sure as heck beat cleaning.

With Zane in her life, Anita thought dazedly, reclining limply back on the bed as his forceful sucks continued, she wouldn't have to worry about falling asleep at night. He'd have her so worn out it would be all she could to do to keep her eyes open during the day. She'd also have a pigsty for a home and an energy bill to rival Rockefeller Center at the holidays. Not to mention be disowned by her parents.

Regardless of how her parents might perceive him, Zane in her life wasn't an option. Tonight was a one-time thing. A single outing into the land of forbidden fantasies with a man who believed she experimented with this type of pleasure everyday. Tomorrow she'd be back to boring old Anita, picking imaginary dust bunnies in the wee hours of the morning.

Zane's mouth left her body, and she whimpered in protest. She was about to push him back into position when he lifted his head and flashed a wicked grin. He licked his lips, his eyes brilliant blue with untamed desire. "You taste sweet, princess. I'm going to eat you all up, every inch of you."

Before she could even tell him how fantastic that sounded, he palmed her thighs with his strong hands and buried his dark head back between her legs. His lips rubbed over her clit just once, then latched onto the swollen nub and pulled. Every thought in her mind scattered with the unexpected and soul-shattering tug. Arching up, she drove her short nails into his scalp and ground her pussy hard against his seeking mouth. She didn't know how he could breathe, she had him trapped so completely, and she really didn't care.

He tugged at her clit again, this time with his teeth, and her entire body shuddered in delicious response. She gripped his hair harder, hanging onto his ears for dear life as he alternately licked and sucked and bit at her distended, shivering clit.

The orgasm that had been hovering from the moment she'd first buried her fingers inside her slick, damp core, pitched through her, tightening each muscle and cell to a crescendo of burning need. His sucks grew faster, his hands gripped her thighs harder, and as she flew to the zenith of ecstasy, she cried out his name.

"Zane! Oh, God, yes! Don't stop!"

He continued to eat at her, licking away the come that lathered his lips and tongue until the shivers left her body and she fell boneless to the bed. Placing a kiss at her center, Zane lifted from between her legs and moved to stand beside the bed. He took her hand and pulled her to the edge of the bed as well, then swiveled her and settled her feet on the floor.

Anita stared at him through a haze, wanting to say something. Thank you. That was incredible. Did he think they could do it again soon? The selfishness of the last thought reached her and she frowned at him. She hadn't yet had her turn to pleasure him. Why on earth was he making them get up already?

Fighting for breath, she asked, "What about you?"

He chuckled and looked down at his cock, standing proud and thick amidst the dark, furled hair between his muscular legs. "Don't worry, he's not going anywhere. I just thought a change in scenery might be nice, and maybe a little food."

She could eat. She hadn't eaten dinner after all. And who knew what time it was, or what day for that matter. With a nod of agreement, she came to her feet and started to follow him from the room. His discarded jeans and boxers caught her attention and on impulse she bent and hung them loosely over the end of the bed. She'd started to follow a second time when her own cast aside clothes came into view.

A gasp of disbelief slipped past her lips at her carelessness. Good gracious, she'd only known the man a short while and he'd not only rocked her universe twice, but he'd turned her in to a slob!

"How can anyone live this way," she muttered, bending for her shirt and bra. A loud grunt halted her mid-stretch, and she straightened and met Zane's glare.

"Don't," he uttered sharply.

Anita frowned at his words. She had to have heard him wrong. He couldn't want her to leave the room in chaos. "What did you say?"

"I said, don't touch my stuff."

Okay, so she hadn't heard him wrong. Still, he couldn't like his things tossed about with absolutely no order. Mindless of her nakedness, she placed her hands at her hips and searched for a rational argument. When nothing came to her, she asked, "Do you enjoy living in a pigsty?"

"It's not a pigsty," he corrected in a calmer tone, scanning the area around them, "but, yes, I like my stuff lying around."

*"Why?"*

He shrugged, his sweaty muscles bunching. "Because…because it makes it feel more homey. You're a woman, you ought to know about stuff like that."

Maybe she ought to, but she didn't. She couldn't remember her house feeling homey once in her entire life, not even when she'd lived with her parents. Their place had been then, as it was now, pristine to a fault. Never an ounce of clutter to be found. Even as a child she knew better than to leave things lying around. Her mother was constantly saying how company could stop by at any moment and if they saw her stuff out and about they'd know what a disorderedly mess she was.

Those words had made sense for so long. Could it be they weren't accurate? Was it even possible that chaos and coziness could go hand in hand?

Skeptical over something she'd always taken for granted, Anita glanced past Zane to where voices sounded in the main room. "What about the T.V.?"

He shook his head and narrowed his gaze. "What about it?"

"Why do you leave it on when you aren't watching it?"

He looked hesitant, then finally answered. "Noise. I don't care for living alone. I even leave it on while I sleep. Lost power once and I didn't sleep the rest of the night."

Oh, Lord, is this what was wrong with her? She was too neat to ever be completely happy, and too alone to sleep at night? It made sense on so many levels. The one and only time she remembered sleeping through the night was the weekend Jordan stayed at her place. Her friend's clothes had filled the house, as her voice did the air.

How improbable was that? She, Ms. Prim and Proper herself, needed chaos and noise. What's more, it took a near stranger to point it out.

Speaking of Zane, why was he living alone in a cabin nestled in the middle of nowhere? For someone who knew they disliked solitude it didn't make a bit of sense. "If you don't like being alone, why aren't you married?"

His expression turned from confused to cold in an instant. His body visibly tensing, he crossed his arms over his chest and took a menacing step toward her. "Because that way no one touches my stuff. Now are we going to play twenty questions or are we going to fuck?"

Anita's breath caught at his gruff words and even gruffer tone. She fumbled for a response, but couldn't think past the mad pounding of her heart, or the callousness of his sinister glare. Obviously, it was time to go. Before his mood got any blacker.

She turned and made a hasty grab for her shirt. Yanking it over her head, she murmured, "I have to go."

His snicker rang cruel and mocking to her ears. "What's the matter Naughty Nita, afraid to stick around and play like a big girl?"

"No," she denied, vehemently shaking her head at his narrowed gaze. Every part of her wanted to stay here and play like a big girl. She had anyway until the Zane she was slowly coming to know turned into one she never saw coming. Was the man who'd called for a dominatrix in the first place the one who stood before her now? And if it was and she did stay, what would he expect of her?

His scowl retreated slightly, but not enough for the tension to leave her body. "If you aren't leaving, I suggest you lose the shirt and take a seat on the couch, while I grab some food and a couple of beers."

"I don't drin…" She stopped short as his scowl turned to a knowing smirk.

He chuckled, the sound dry and nearly as mocking as the last time. "You don't drink. You don't get naked with your *many* men. And my guess is you don't swear unless someone pushes your limits the way I've been doing. How the hell can a girl claim a name like Naughty Mistress Nita and have so few bad habits?"

Anita's anxiety turned to annoyance with his too close to home accusation. Damn it, she was tired of always being the good girl, the one who consistently followed the rules and stayed inside the lines, the one who ran when things got a little too hot to handle. At least for tonight, she was through with the running. She'd already made her mind up to spend this night indulging in the sort of wild pleasures she could only before dream of, and that's exactly what she planned to do. His foul mood be damned.

Pulling bravado from a reserve she'd only just realized existed, she took a step forward, looked Zane squarely in the eye and lied. "That isn't what I was going to say. I drink. In fact, I could probably drink you under the table."

He shot her a look that said he didn't believe her for a minute, then with a parting smirk, made his way to the open kitchen.

\* \* \* \* \*

Zane yanked the cap off his beer bottle with a furious twist. He swallowed the cold ale, relishing the way it cooled his warm, dry throat. Now if it would just work on cooling his temper. He hadn't meant to lash out at Anita like that, but damn it, did she have to ask about his marriage? She hadn't come right out and asked about it, but she'd asked why he wasn't married, and it'd been more than enough to get his hackles up.

It had also been enough to turn her face white as a ghost. She'd been back to looking sixteen at that moment when she spun away from him and hastily tugged on her shirt. The panicked look in her eyes assured him that she was intent on leaving. He didn't want her to go. And not just so they could fuck the way he'd suggested, but because it had been too damned long since he'd spent time with a woman.

He should answer her questions right now, explain he was separated and nearly divorced, only he didn't want Trina coming into play tonight. He wanted this to be about him and Anita. Just one night of pleasure, a distraction from the harsh realities of everyday life. The fact that Anita stayed after all that had been said told him she wanted the same thing.

He looked across the low counter to where she sat wrapped up in an old throw blanket on the couch. She appeared to be watching TV. He'd bet his favorite T-square she wasn't paying attention to the show that played. Rather, she was waiting for him to sit down, expectant of the way he'd act when he did.

Refusing to keep her in suspense, Zane popped the remains of last night's spaghetti into the microwave and set the timer. He grabbed both of their beers and crossed to the small sitting area. The floorboards of the old cabin creaked when he'd nearly reached Anita, and she visibly jumped as she turned to look at him. Hesitance rested in her gaze and her mouth turned down slightly at the corners.

She looked doleful and innocent, and he fought the urge to haul her into his arms and apologize for acting like an asshole. He shouldn't feel so badly about his behavior, not considering their situation. If she acted the way he'd presumed a dominatrix should, he wouldn't be feeling like a heel at all. Of course, if she acted the way he'd always thought a dominatrix would — sticking around long enough to beat the shit out of him, take his money, then run — he wouldn't be standing here buck naked, anticipating the night still to come.

Rounding the couch, Zane set his beer on the coffee table. He uncapped hers and handed it to her. She stared at the bottle as if unsure how to proceed, and he recalled her earlier words about not drinking. She'd taken them back, but her retraction had been about as believable as her statement she could drink him under the table. If nothing else, she was adorable when she got all fired up that way, color flaring in her high cheekbones and her freckles all but glowing.

Adorable and high-strung, and nothing at all like a dominatrix.

He had to quit coming back to that. Even if it were Anita's first night on the job, it didn't change what she was. Or the reason she was here. At least why she'd come here initially. That reason sure as hell wasn't to bond over idle conversation about his housekeeping or sleeping habits, or for that matter his marital status.

But then, why'd she ask so damned many questions about his personal life?

"Thanks."

The softly spoken word and the gentle tug on his fingers as she took the beer from him pulled Zane from his musings. He watched in silence as she brought the bottle to her mouth and swallowed a sip. Her nose crinkled and her eyes widened for an instant, but other than that she made no signs she was averse to its taste.

Leaning forward, she set her beer next to his. The blanket slipped from her right shoulder as she moved, exposing a small, firm breast with a large, puckered nipple. She sat back and tugged the blanket back up, but not quickly enough to stop his mind from wandering or his cock from zinging to life all over again.

Their gazes locked on his erect shaft in unison. He looked from his penis to Anita's face, half expecting to see a blush. Instead, he saw a smile. He grinned back on impulse, drawn in by the way the expression animated her entire face and lit up her eyes.

"You sure you can wait to eat?" she asked lightly.

He chuckled, baffled once more by her unexpected response. She had to be the single most difficult woman to understand that he'd ever met. "I think so," he said, with another glance at his cock, "but he seems to have a mind of his own. "

Her smile blossomed further, and the carefree sensation that had settled over him was enveloped by a mega-dose of guilt. "Look, I'm sorry about before. I just don't make a habit of sharing my personal life."

Her mouth fell flat, but the hint of tranquility remained in her eyes. "It isn't important, Zane. I should never have asked you so many questions in the first place."

"You're right, it's not important. Not at all. What is important is getting some food in your body. I'd hate to see you get tired out when I've only just begun."

Anita's smile returned in full force. Her voice sounded way too serious for Zane's comfort when she spoke next. "I'd hate that too. Especially since I haven't even had a chance to break out the whips and chains."

He swallowed hard against a sudden spurt of anxiety, and hoped like hell she was only kidding.

# Chapter Six

&

Anita set her empty beer bottle on the scarred coffee table behind them, then sank back to the floor and into Zane's arms. Though it had taken every bit of willpower he possessed, he'd put off touching her the entire time they'd eaten. He couldn't wait any longer. Not when he knew how quickly her lone beer had gone to her head. Her language had gone from sweet to downright colorful, and if she had any lasting worry over his adverse behavior, then she'd long since forgotten about it.

She rolled onto him, crushing her breasts between them and gyrated her damp sex against his groin. A groan escaped his lips, and she laughed throatily.

"I hope you're finished with your food, Zane. Naughty Nita needs to feel your great big cock in her pussy." She slipped her hand beneath the blanket covering them, and a sucking sound reached his ears as she stroked her juicy mound. "I'm so wet for you, baby." She pulled her hand back up and placed her damp fingers against the seam of his lips. "Taste how hot you make me."

Her words were half demand, half throaty plea. He wasn't about to deny either. Parting his mouth, he sucked her slippery fingers in and licked at her salty essence. The knowledge she delivered the juices that warmed his tongue made her musky flavor even more potent an aphrodisiac than it had been back on his bed.

"You are wet," he agreed, sucking and feeding from her slender fingers, "and delicious."

She pulled her hand from his mouth and hungrily eyed his lips, licked her own. "What do you think we should do about it?"

"What do you want to do?" he returned, goading her once more into doing the work, speaking her wants aloud, though they were plenty clear in her shimmering amber eyes.

She nipped a kiss at the corner of his mouth, then reared back until her tight, hot body straddled his hard upper thighs. The blanket fell away and her lips tipped with an impish smile as she grasped his erection in her palm. "How about we fuck?"

Zane's blood pumped faster. "Are you sure?"

"Oh yeah." She squeezed his cock harder, strumming its inflamed length with the softness of her small hand. He shuddered within her firm grasp and her smile grew. "He wants to fuck too."

He wanted to do something, all right. But despite his earlier proclamation, fucking wasn't his style. At least, not with a woman like Anita. Or at least the woman he believed her to be. "How about we have mountain shaking sex instead?" he asked, twining his fingers through her chaotic hair.

"Sounds good to me." She dropped her mouth to his chest and licked at his flat nipples, probing the ends with her rough tongue until they grew taut. With her hand, she continued to squeeze and tease his hot, hard penis. He sank his fingers farther into her tousled hair, fearing he'd yank it out altogether from the bittersweet tension. Either that or burst free of the thin skin covering his pulsing erection.

He could climax so easily right now, but he wouldn't allow himself to come in her palm. He could achieve that sort of satisfaction on his own. What he needed tonight was to be deeply buried in Anita's spasming pussy when he came, to milk the tremors from her body with his own. He needed it soon, he realized. Fast, hot release just once. The rest of this night they'd take things slow. Experience. Savor. And grant each other's wildest fantasies. And she would stay through the night. Of that he had no doubt.

Pulling her into his arms, Zane rolled them until she lay flat on her back and gaped up at him. He sat back on his haunches and feasted on the sight of her wide eyes and altogether surprised expression. Her sable curls appeared almost red in the firelight, her toned, tight body smooth and flawless save for a handful of freckles. Her pussy gleamed, already so wet from her own touch, soon to be twice as wet from his.

Her surprise passed, she held out her arms impatiently. "Are you coming?"

"Not yet, princess," he said wryly, purposefully misunderstanding her. "But soon." They'd both be coming damn soon if he had his way.

She giggled at his quip, and he silenced the sound with his mouth. Plunging past her lips, he fed off her sweetness, devouring with explosively deep and intense thrusts. He squeezed her ripe breasts, twisting her nipples until she moaned against his mouth and rocked her slit against his throbbing shaft. The head of his cock rimmed her swollen cleft and he felt the moisture that already drenched her eager lips.

"Take me now, Zane!" Anita cried, breaking free of his mouth. "Fuck me, please."

Yes, that's what he wanted. Not callous, cold fucking, but rough, pleasurable fucking. It was possible to fuck someone you cared for. He'd just never realized it until now. "Do you have any condoms?" he asked hoarsely.

Her seeking hips stopped and she stared at him, wide-eyed. *"What?"*

"We need protection."

Her eyes edged wider. "But…shit…I don't have any!"

Zane nearly laughed at the horror in her words and that written on her face. Instead, he tweaked her nipple and said teasingly, "Imagine that, a mistress who doesn't drink or carry condoms."

"Damn it, I do drink! And I told you I'm not supposed to sleep with you."

"You don't drink. If you did, your eyes wouldn't look glassy after one beer." Not to mention her sudden bout with foul mouth syndrome. "As for your job limitations, let's just say you're going to get a big, fat tip for all your hard work." Before she could say another word, he bent and took her mouth with a bone-liquefying kiss. With effort, he pulled back when he felt himself sinking too far in. He let go any more and it'd be far too late for a condom.

"I'll be right back," he promised with one more brush of his lips, and then made haste for the bedroom, fervently praying he had a condom. Better yet ten. The night was young, and he felt just as youthful. Able to go all night. Or at least as long as Anita could hold out.

\* \* \* \* \*

He hadn't been lying about giving her a tip, Anita realized when Zane returned a few minutes later. He was going to give her a big, fat purple-headed pulsating tip. And she'd never been more excited and, possibly, more tipsy in her life.

He made quick work of rolling the condom on, and then he was covering her with his strong, sexy body. The head of his long, thick cock brushed against the opening of her swollen pussy, and she drew in a sharp breath of anticipation.

"Now!" she cried out, barely recognizing the needy voice as her own.

"Yes, now," he growled back, bracing his hands on either side of her face.

He plunged into her with one solid, possessive thrust. She cried out in ecstasy as he filled her hot, eager body with his hard, impressive sex. And then his mouth was on hers, stormy, demanding, needing so much. Everything she wanted to give him. And everything she wanted to get back in return.

Zane's fingers melded into the supple flesh of her thighs as he thrust again and again into her welcoming body, driving her higher and higher. But not high enough. She needed all this, and yet she needed more. She needed control.

Breaking free of his powerful mouth and forceful tongue, Anita kicked against the floor and brought them spinning around until she rode him the way she'd longed to do since the moment she'd awoken to her dream lover. Only Zane wasn't a dream, he was a real live man. And what a man he was — virile, rugged, slightly untamed, and beautiful if such a thing could be said about someone as masculine as he.

She rocked her hips slowly against him and smiled down at his passion-clouded gaze, loving the feel of total and complete control. Here, atop Zane Matthews, she felt sexy for the first time in her life. Actually, she'd felt sexy since the moment they'd met. Not boring, not conservative, not plain old Anita, daughter of a small-town minister and his goody two shoes wife. But hot and wanted.

"Are you going to dominate me now, Anita?" Zane breathed harshly.

That's exactly what she wanted to do. Dominate him, make him beg for her touch, make him explode with desire. "I'm going to make you beg," she purred.

He grinned arrogantly. "Is that so? And what should I beg for, princess?"

"Deep."

He raised a dark eyebrow. "I want to go deep, do I?"

"Yes," she rasped, refusing to be shy now, but allow the liquid courage strumming through her veins to guide her every word, her every move. "You want to bury your cock so deep into my pussy I can't breathe. You want to make me come until we're both soaked with it, and then you want me to make you come too."

He chuckled throatily, hungrily. "I want all that?"

She wasn't about to be offended by his laughter. She knew he wanted all that and then some, the proof was embedded deep into her core. It would be even deeper in a second. "Damn right you do. Tilt your hips, Zane. Take me deep."

"Like this?" He lifted his pelvis, and Anita bit back her whimper at the pleasure pain quaking through her soul.

"Oh, yeah...like that." He moved again, and she couldn't stop the helpless mewl that tripped from her lips. "Oh, God, right there! Now, now...move." He did, rocking his ridged swollen cock against her slippery vulva, increasing the friction and speed in turn until his balls slapped loudly against her ass, and she squealed in sure delight.

Anita dug her nails into the muscled flesh of his forearms, mindless to their surroundings, mindless to everything but Zane. And even he was getting foggy. His face anyway. The rest of him she was more than little aware of. He slowed the erratic pace as their breathing grew heavy and the air tainted with dewy warmth and heady sex. She growled her displeasure, biting her nails harder into his flesh.

"Keep going," she ordered. "Faster! Make me dizzy."

"Where do my hands go?" Zane demanded, his words strained and his eyes dark as midnight with lust.

"On my ass. Dig your nails into my ass."

His short nails scraped into her buttocks, and she squeaked out her delight. "Ohhh...baby...that's right."

She pumped against him, no longer caring about control. She was beyond control. Now she just needed, needed to find the release that welled in her, stronger than she'd ever experienced. Needed to feel him climaxing inside her. She needed him.

"If we don't slow down I'm going to come," Zane rasped, his muscles grown taut beneath her hands, and his cock pulsating thick and strong inside her slick folds.

"I can't stop," she cried, increasing the frantic pace, grinding her soaked pussy against his hard pelvis, breathing in the smell of their mingled sex. Even if she could stop, she wouldn't. This was too good. No, they were too good.

"I can't stop," she breathed again harshly, as the first wave of the orgasm shook through her, shuddering her limbs, making her dizzy just the way she'd asked for. She convulsed around his hard cock, and she felt him spasm in return.

His shaft pressed against her clit, and she drove her nails into his skin as far they could go. "Ohhh...oh...Zane ...ohmigod!"

"Oh yeah," he shouted back, milking her with the force of his frenzied movements. "Ah, fuck, Anita. Don't stop now, princess." His large hands cupped her ass fully, and he dragged her down onto his solid chest, roared into her ear. "Yeah, keep moving. Keep moving. Oh yeah...oh hell...ohhh...damn."

The last of his thrusts died down, and Anita crumpled the remainder of the way onto him, drinking in the rapid beat of his heart. She should be trying to breathe right now, but all she could do was smile. Lord, she felt good. In a way that had nothing to do with the single beer she'd drank. The buzz she rode now was that of a completely different kind. One that she couldn't even put into words.

"Good," Zane uttered amid hasty pants.

She laughed. That was sure one way to put it. "Good."

He cupped her bottom and pressed a kiss to her temple. "Better next time."

Hmm...next time. That sounded better than good for sure. Only she shouldn't stick around for a next time, she realized, her smile falling flat. Of course, the slowly swelling bulge against her belly made leaving all the more difficult.

What were the odds of her getting to partake in this sort of activity again? At least anytime soon and with someone as skilled and giving as Zane? There were no odds. Because it wouldn't happen. Certainly, not around her hometown.

Just one more time. One shot at the infamous second round. Then she would gather up her things, get in her car, and return to her too damned neat house and too damned boring lifestyle.

Anita lifted her head and met Zane's eyes. He flashed her a lazy but smug grin. "I don't know why that frown's on your face, but I bet I can turn it upside down."

She laughed lightly, appreciating his easy goading more than he could ever know. No one had ever teased her the way he did. It made her feel special. A lot like the way she felt when he pressed his magical mouth against hers and heated her up from the inside out.

Knowing just how upset he became the moment she delved into personal territory, she shook away her thoughts, and teased her fingers along his rough beard, traced the strong contour of his jaw. "You think so, huh?"

"Umm hmm...just watch me."

She did watch, and gasped aloud at his next move. Gathering her tightly in his arms, Zane came to his feet and started across the room.

"Where are we going?" she asked, though it was more than a little obvious by the fact there was only one other room in the cabin big enough to fit them both.

"Bed," he said without pausing.

Her heart beat faster. "But—"

"But nothing." He cleared the bedroom doorway, flipped on the light, and looked down at her. There was nearly as much integrity in his deep blue gaze as there was passion. "I told you I've only just begun, Anita. Before the morning comes there won't be a chance in hell of you forgetting me."

Gracious, he sounded so sure of himself. And she believed him. And that was bad. She hadn't come here to have someone imprinted on her mind. Least of all someone she could never again have after tonight. "I can't stay!"

"You can," he corrected sharply. "And you will."

And she wanted to. But still... "I shouldn't."

He nodded, amusement flashing in his eyes. "Trust me, princess, you should."

"Why do you want me to?"

The mirth faded from Zane's eyes as he placed her onto his bed. "Because...because it's storming outside, and I know just how badly the roads wash out around here in severe weather. You won't make it more than a mile and you'll be running back here for help to get your car out of the mud. In other words, you're doing us both a favor by staying."

Was that really why? For some reason Anita didn't believe him. She also knew better than to question his reasoning. Especially when he was using that logic to convince her to spend an entire night in his oh-so-capable arms.

Heaven help her, she just couldn't say 'no' to an offer like that.

Apprehension gone, she spread her legs, stretched out her arms, and beckoned him into her embrace. Crawling across the bed on his hands and knees, he sank against her warm, ripe body. His rigid cock settled against her junction, generating heat and moisture deep in her core without any effort at all.

He redoubled his effort then, stroking the length of his tumescent shaft against the quickly swelling flesh of her sex.

She moaned appreciatively, already feeling weightless, boneless from his touch. "You know, you might just have a point, Mr. Matthews."

"Yes, I do," he said wryly, aligning the head of his penis with her opening. "Want to feel it?"

She couldn't stop the throaty laugh that rolled past her lips. Nipping a kiss at the corner of his mouth, she nodded her agreement. "All right. You win. Show Naughty Nita exactly why God gave you that point."

# Chapter Seven

စာ

Zane woke to warm, supple limbs tangled around his body, and a smile claimed his lips. Absently, he ran a hand over the woman's narrow back.

Trina, he thought groggily. No, definitely not Trina. His ex-wife didn't sleep with her arms and legs wrapped around him. She sure as hell didn't sleep naked, or smell like fresh cut flowers. Or snore like a banshee, he added when a low, rumbling sound reverberated off his chest.

Anita, he recalled, his smile turning into a grin. His cute little dominatrix lover. Much more emphasis on the former than the latter.

He shouldn't have asked her to stay last night—even though she hadn't pressed him for reasoning beyond a simple 'why', he'd been able to see the questions in her eyes. And why shouldn't she be puzzled, considering the way he'd lashed out at her the moment she asked about his personal life? Staying over, sharing a man's bed was about as personal as two people could get.

She might be confused, but he wasn't one bit sorry for his actions. He also wasn't above convincing her to spend a few more hours with him. He'd realized it last night, and he knew it more so now. She was the distraction he'd been in need of. The warm, willing woman he needed to take his mind off his problems for a few more, much-deserved hours.

And she definitely *could* do just that, he thought when she shifted against him, her pelvis brushing against his groin and waking up his cock in an instant. His hand stilled on her back, and he groaned out his response to her accidental brush.

Anita shifted against him again, eliciting yet another low moan. Then, finally coming awake, she gasped and lifted her head. With her amber eyes wide and her freckled nose scrunched up she looked young, adorable and completely disoriented. Obviously, she wasn't used to waking up in a stranger's bed. Good.

"Morning, princess," Zane said, his voice gruff. He restarted the movement of his hand over her back, this time taking the slow strokes further down to the swell of her ass. "Sleep well?"

She arched against his palm each time his hand journeyed to her buttocks, her eyes darkening with rampant lust. Clearly, he wasn't the only one affected by their nearness.

In a voice filled with both awe and passion, she murmured, "Actually, yes. I did."

"And that's surprising?" he questioned, bringing his hand up to glide through the ends of her short, chaotic curls. He lifted his head off the pillow and brushed his mouth over hers. She tasted sinfully sweet even first thing in the morning.

She sighed as he pulled back. "I have trouble sleeping."

Funny, she hadn't seemed to have a single problem sleeping last night. At least not falling asleep. The moment they'd stopped teasing each other, she'd been out.

Once more Zane met her lips, this time running his tongue over the full lower one. Anita mewled quietly, the helpless, erotic sound striking a chord of desire deep within him. He sailed his hands down her back and cupped her taut ass. The need to bury his cock into her silken folds hit him like a wrecking ball.

"Maybe you just needed someone to wear you out," he growled.

Her lips took on the impish smile he'd already come to know well. "Maybe."

He gripped her cheeks more firmly, grinding her damp pussy against his thick shaft. "Maybe I should wear you out again."

She opened her mouth, and he awaited her eager reply. Instead, she closed it and glanced around the bedroom. Her smile was gone when she looked back at him, and for a moment his hopes for the day before them wavered. Then, she placed her hands on his chest and pushed herself into a kneeling position.

Zane waited expectantly, wondering what she planned to do in that pose, conjuring up a number of things that would suit him just fine. Only she didn't do any of them, but moved to the side of the bed, taking his comforter with her. Without a word, she wrapped the blanket around her slender shoulders and stood.

The hope that had faltered before now sank altogether, and he stared at her in disbelief. "Where are you going?"

Anita didn't look back as she crossed the room and reached for her rumpled slacks. "I need to get dressed."

No. She needed to come back to bed so they could indulge in some early morning fun. "Why?" he asked, sitting up in the bed and scooting back against the knotty-pine headboard. "What's the big rush?"

"I need to get home."

"Oh." Of course, she had to go home. What the fuck was he thinking? He was lucky she'd stayed as long as she had, not to mention shared her body with him.

"Do you have to?" The words left his mouth before Zane could stop them. The look she flashed him ensured she was just as shocked by his question.

"What?"

Shit, he'd already said it, what was the point of taking it back? The odds they would see each other again were next to nil, he might as well press his luck.

Zane put on his best pleading face, which wasn't too good considering how seldom he used it. "It's Saturday morning, princess, and I don't have anywhere to go. Unless you do, I think you should stay awhile longer."

"You want me to stay?" she all but gasped. Clutching the comforter tightly to her chest, she narrowed her gaze. "Why? What would we do?"

Some more of what they did last night, only with some new and exciting twists? Judging by Anita's knit brow that answer wouldn't go over too well. He shrugged. "Hell, I don't know. Have some breakfast and…go fishing?"

Her face paled, and she glanced across the room to the doorway. "You want me to use that pole on you, right?" Shaking her head disapprovingly, she looked back at him. "I'm sorry, Zane, but that was last night's offer, today you're on your own."

"Huh?" The pole? What the hell was she—oh! He chuckled as realization set in. No, he didn't want her to take after him with a goddamned fishing pole. "I meant really go fishing. The rain's slowed up, and they tend to bite well in this weather." Okay, they hadn't bitten worth a damn in this weather last night, but she didn't need to know that.

She tipped her head to the side, scrunched up her nose and frowned. "You really want to take me fishing?"

He had until she looked at him like it was the worst idea she'd ever heard. "Don't get into that kind of thing, huh?"

"No. I mean, I've never tried. I really have no idea if I'd like it or—why do you want me to stay?"

He could almost hear the wheels spinning in her head. If he'd confused her last night, then he had doubly so now. And, really, that only seemed fair given he wasn't any longer sure of his rationale. Keeping her around to fuck was one thing, but taking her fishing? Hell, he didn't even share his favorite sport with the guys.

He shrugged again. "I guess I thought you might enjoy some time away."

"It sounds fun, really, but I just can't do it. I need to call Jordan, and—"

Anita stopped short when he climbed out of the bed. He heard her sharp intake of breath as her gaze traveled the length of his naked body. She stilled on his engorged erection, and her face turned a blistering red.

She mouthed, "Oh my gracious."

Zane just barely contained his laughter. The irony of her reaction had his doubts about her profession resurfacing anew. He refused to bring the subject up now, when she looked ready to turn tail and run.

Pretending he hadn't noticed her response, he crossed to the dresser, picked up his cell phone, and tossed it to her. Her eyes flew wide as she made a hasty grab for the phone. The comforter she wore like a protective shield fell to the floor.

He murmured his gratefulness as her lithe body was exposed to his view, her small breasts jiggling enticingly with her movements. That hadn't been his intention, but it worked pretty damned well.

The phone clasped in her hand, Anita grabbed for the blanket and hurriedly wrapped it around her. He would've loved to ask what the hell she thought she was hiding, but thought better of it.

"Use my cell phone," he said when she'd finished securing herself in the makeshift cocoon. "You have to walk down the path to get a signal, but it works well enough."

Zane waited for her refusal, figured it a guarantee given her behavior, but she did just the opposite.

"All right. I'll stay, but just for a few more hours."

"Great," he said quickly, before she could change her mind. He opened the second dresser drawer and pulled out a flannel shirt. He thought about tossing it to her, but deciding that trick would only work once, crossed to her and held it out. "I don't have any jeans, but this ought to be more comfortable for your top half anyway."

Accepting it, Anita nodded. "Yeah. I don't own any jeans either."

"What?"

"Nothing. Give me a few minutes to change and call Jordan."

* * * * *

"I don't own any jeans either." Anita repeated her earlier words in disgust as she made her way down the forest path, a fine mist dampening the air.

Considering he'd worn jeans yesterday, it was obvious Zane meant he didn't have any jeans that would fit her, not that he didn't own any altogether. And like the stiff-dressed, conservative woman she was, she responded by telling him she didn't own any jeans. What a moron.

It was nearly as bad as admitting she'd not only never shared her bed with a man, but she'd never seen one naked. At least not in the light of day and judging by his engorged penis, completely aroused. True, she'd seen that same man rock-hard and fondling himself last night, but at the time she'd been too excited to fully comprehend everything. And later—she'd only drunk one beer, but it must have gone straight to her head. She had not only crawled into bed with him, she'd slept naked!

She didn't even need her parents around to tell her how sacrilegious that was, it was common logic because of the fact that pajamas had been invented. If God wanted people to sleep naked, then that never would've happened.

Naked or not, she'd slept through the night for the first time in years. No bad dreams about her mother hounding her to do this or that, no nightmares where her father lectured her relentlessly about decorum and how far she fell from the goodness tree. Just sleep. Sound, peaceful sleep that was concluded the moment she felt a large, warm, slightly rough hand caressing her back and the top of her buttocks.

"Mmm…Zane," she murmured, recalling just how quickly her body liquefied under his touch.

If she hadn't been so worried about getting out of his cabin before he realized what a mistake he'd made, that she was nothing at all like the woman he wanted, she would have surrendered to his hands. She would gladly have given in to the massive hard-on pressed up against her cleft, pooling moistness deep inside her core.

Even if it had been wrong of her to stay the night, Anita couldn't feel sorry about it. Just like she couldn't feel sorry for agreeing to spend a few more hours with him. She didn't understand his reasoning for asking her to stay, but given the way he'd acted when she probed too deeply the night before, she wouldn't push him to explain. She'd simply relish their morning together.

And maybe, she thought, turning her head to the side and inhaling Zane's woodsy scent on the flannel shirt, if she could muster up the courage, she'd let Naughty Mistress Nita have a few more minutes of playtime.

\* \* \* \* \*

"You got it," Zane said, watching intently as Anita held tight to her fishing pole. Something had been toying with her bait for over fifteen minutes now. He'd be willing to bet that something was a pint-sized Blue Gill or a no-flavor Rock Bass, both of which he'd toss back if she ever landed them. Given the healthy glow in her cheeks and the merriment in her eyes, he wasn't about to point that out.

"Now, wait just a second," he said, when the fish took her bobber part way under again. Finally, the red and white floater sank beneath the surface. "Okay, now jerk. That's it, princess, reel 'em in."

"He feels big!" she said with all the exuberance of a child on Christmas morning.

He bit back his chuckle. Could be because he'd set the drag to next to nothing. A minnow was liable to feel big. "Probably a monster. Just keep reeling."

The tiniest of tails broke the surface when the fish had nearly reached the shore.

"Oh, it's just a baby," Anita muttered, reeling it in the rest of the way. She angled the tip of the pole toward Zane, and he caught the slippery Blue Gill in his hand. He could sense the sorrow in Anita's eyes even before he lifted his head and met her stricken gaze. God, she looked like she'd run over a kitten.

Catching her bottom lip between her teeth, she frowned at the fish. "He's so cute, Zane. I didn't hurt him, did I?"

"No, princess. You didn't hurt him. As soon as I put 'em in the water, he's going to go back to his mommy and daddy." He slipped the hook from the Blue Gill's mouth and tossed him back into the water. The fish immediately disappeared from sight. Relieved she really hadn't hurt him, Zane looked back at her.

"See that? Right about now his daddy's grounding him for swimming beyond the limits."

She laughed, the sadness in her eyes replaced with a humor that lit her entire face and did a razzle-dazzle number on his heart the likes of which he could've never seen coming. "You're making fun of me, aren't you?" she asked softly.

He had been, but not anymore. Now he couldn't think about anything beyond kissing her senseless. "Do you really think I would do something like that?"

She nodded, her short, sable curls bouncing in a way that made his hands itch to reach out, grab a handful, and yank her mouth to his. "Yes. I think you would."

"All right. Maybe I was just a little, but you look adorable when you get all riled up. It makes me want to kiss you. Only I probably couldn't stop with just one kiss, I'd want more. I'd want to suck on those big nipples of yours. The ones you wouldn't let me see this morning. Then I'd go lower, and lick at your sweet little pussy. And of course I couldn't just stop there. I'd have to have all of you."

Anita's mouth went slack and she swallowed audibly. "Maybe if you want to do all that—maybe you should."

He nodded, held rapt by the sight of her luscious lips. "Maybe I will."

"Maybe you should wash your hands first."

He jerked his gaze back to her eyes and chuckled. "Don't like fish slime?"

Her nose crinkled. "I've never tasted it, but I doubt it."

And he doubted he could stop from holding her, kissing her, or touching her, when her freckled little nose was scrunched up like that. Without a second thought, he closed the short space between them and focused on her unpainted lips. She swallowed hard again. He ignored the sound and took the last step toward her, the one that had their bodies touching, her breasts rubbing against the hard planes of his chest.

Her breathing sped up as he slanted his head. His own jerked from his body in rapid spasms, far more rapidly than what he should be feeling over something so simple as a kiss. Only he wasn't sure what was happening here was simple any longer. At least, he didn't feel like it was.

A throaty sigh broke from Anita's lips, and he bent his head to taste her. Their lips had barely brushed when thunder rumbled loudly overhead and the rain that had been on hiatus fell down in cold, fat drops.

Zane pulled away with a curse. He straightened and glared up at the dark sky.

So much for whatever was about to happen. He wasn't going to stand out here and have a repeat performance of yesterday. Of course, his soaking wet trip back to the cabin had ended with waking Sleeping Beauty via a less than conventional but oh-so-enjoyable means. Still, he didn't want her getting sick.

He glanced back at her lips one last time and then raised his gaze to her passion-hazed eyes. Damn it, she looked eager for some action. Hopefully she'd still be ready by the time they returned to the cabin. "Let me wash up, and we'll head back before it gets any worse."

When she didn't respond, he squatted near the edge of the lake and scrubbed his hands together in the cool water. He was about to stand when her arms wrapped around him from behind and she placed a kiss as soft as air at his nape. Soft, and yet so arousing by its unexpected occurrence.

Anita's rough tongue moved to his ear and rimmed the lobe, her teeth nipped lightly at the thin skin beneath. The blood burst through his body with her subtle caress, rekindling his morning erection and hardening it further. There was something intoxicating about her. Something that he'd never felt with a woman before. There had to be or his cock wouldn't be so painfully hard from such a simple touch.

Maybe it was a trick the dominatrix side of her knew. "What are you doing?"

"Experimenting," she murmured huskily.

"With what?"

"I don't know."

Whatever it was, it was working.

Kneeling on the wet grass, Zane turned in her embrace and held her at arm's length to see her expression. His gaze darted to where her nipples thrust hard against the flannel shirt. It was more than evident she hadn't put on her bra. It was even more obvious the sex goddess he'd encountered last night was back at full throttle.

Damn, he wanted her. Wanted to fuck her right here beside the lake with the storm streaming down upon them and Mother Nature witnessing their every move.

The wind picked up, pelting them with cold, hard bullets of rain. Common sense played at the fringes of his mind. They really needed to head back to the cabin, to find dry clothes. It would be a hell of a lot easier to listen to that rationale if Anita looked cold. But she didn't. No, she looked hot, willing and sexy as hell.

He stroked the back of his knuckles along her cheek. "You're getting wet, princess."

She nodded, drawing herself back against his chest, until their bodies were flush and her lips so very near to his own. "Hmm mmm…and it isn't from the rain."

# Chapter Eight

## ဆ

"We should go back to the cabin."

Anita knew Zane was right on some level, but that wasn't the level that was shivering with pleasure over the feel of his strong, sensuous mouth on hers. His tongue thrust into her mouth, stroking with wild abandon. She knew that same feeling of desperation, of urgency, felt it in every recess of her body.

"I want you, Zane!" she cried out, uncaring of their surroundings, or who or even what might chance upon them in this open stretch of land and water. "I need you, baby," she rasped, tugging at his lower lip as she pulled away from his mouth. "Do all those things you said you wanted to do. Fuck me in the pouring rain."

His eyes darkened to midnight, and he uttered one word, a single 'yes' before he pushed her back on the damp grass and fiercely popped open the buttons of her shirt. Raw excitement spiked through Anita's body with his animalistic move. She drove her hands beneath his shirt and splayed her palms over his hard, flat abdomen, scrapped her nails against the chiseled muscles.

"Yes, like that, Zane! Tear all my clothes off. Rip them from my body."

With a grunt, he sought out her lips once more. His mouth wasn't gentle as it had been when he kissed her last night, and not even urgent like it had been moments before—now it was forceful and demanding. She tasted his need just as strongly as her own, and met him half way, sucking at his tongue vigorously. With a feral growl, he pulled free of the kiss and worked his way down her neck, eliciting shudders of raw energy as he seared her with his warmth.

Zane laved his tongue over her puckered nipples, and wetness pooled hot and heavy between her thighs. Biting at the skin around her navel, he unzipped her slacks and worked them down her hips, quickly but meticulously.

And not nearly fast enough for Anita's liking. "Faster, Zane. Tear them off. Now."

He gave a short shake of his head and pulled her slacks off the remainder of the way. "You don't have any more pants," he explained when the barrier was gone. A wicked grin stole over his face then and, with a hissing rip, he tore her panties away. He lifted the sodden red and black cotton to his nose and inhaled deeply before tossing it aside. "You don't have any more of those either, but I like you better without."

Anita's heart slammed inside her chest with his move. She liked him better without too — without a single scrap of clothing covering his beautiful flesh.

His large hands fell to her hips and he tipped her pelvis skyward, opened her legs wide to the falling rain. Heat rushed into her face as he gazed so intently at her swollen sex. She fought the sudden urge to clamp her legs tightly together, but then forgot about it completely when he lowered his head to her widespread thighs and sighed loudly.

"Oh, princess, your pussy's soaked." He flicked his finger against her throbbing clit just once, then lowered his head the remainder of the way and coasted his tongue over her labia. With an errant stroke, he thrust hard into her core.

She lurched against his mouth, bucking up wildly with his breathtaking assault, and snagged his overlong hair in her hands. With a furious tug, she wrenched him from between her legs and pinned him with her gaze.

"I want to do that," she said boldly, brazenly, in a voice that was pure demand.

The surprise that had registered on Zane's face when she jerked him up by his hair turned to confusion. "And I'd love to watch you do it, but unless you're a damn good contortionist, it's a physical impossibility."

She laughed throatily, then quickly corrected him. "No. I want to taste *you*, Zane. Let me take your cock into my mouth and make you come."

"Oh." His eyes went wide then, as if her words had only just hit home. "Ohhh… Yes, I'd like that. I'd like that very much."

Rearing back on his knees, he stripped away his clothes. Anita watched as each layer fell to the ground and finally his long, thick penis was set free. Her mouth watered with anticipation as she looked upon the engorged purple head of his cock. Moisture already beaded at the tip. She'd take great pleasure in licking it away, even greater pleasure in creating more of the salty fluid.

Standing long enough to move to her side, he once again came down on his knees. Only he faced the wrong way. He was looking toward the lake, not at her.

"What in Heavens name are you doing?" she asked impatiently.

He flashed a devilish grin over his shoulder. "Lie back and you'll see."

Though she was in no mood for games, she did as he asked, and rested her head on the wet grass. She closed her eyes against the pouring rain, and only opened them again when she felt something soft and smooth brush over her lips.

She gasped at the sight of Zane's strong thighs straddling her face. His cock jutted out mere centimeters from her mouth, telling her exactly what had brushed over her lips. Good Lord, all she had to do was lift her head the tiniest bit, open her mouth, and he'd be inside. How practical.

Zane's tongue darted out, flicking between her legs, deep into the folds of her slippery sex, and she moaned aloud. Oh my gracious, how practical indeed!

"I like this," she breathed, drawing her hand up to wrap around his shaft.

He stopped sucking at her to laugh. "You haven't even started yet."

"I'm going to like it," she corrected, without so much as a single doubt she'd be wrong. She'd liked everything he'd done to her and with her. This would be no exception. "You're going to like it too. As a matter of fact, by the time I'm done there won't be a chance in hell of you forgetting me."

He laughed again, clearly picking up that she'd turned his words from the previous night back on him. "That I have no doubt—" He stopped short and groaned long and loud as Anita fitted her mouth around him, testing his size and flavor.

She pulled back to run her tongue over the small hole at the tip of his penis. The salty, sweet fluid she'd been dying to sample coated her tongue, and she murmured her appreciation. "I do like this, Zane. I can't wait to feel you coming in my mouth."

"Trust me, princess. You keep doing that and you won't be waiting long at all."

"Oh, really?" She licked at that same spot several more times, savoring the way his cock swelled in her hand with each move, then aligned the head of his erection with her mouth and once more took him in. Gently, she cupped his balls as she glided her lips up and down his long, thick shaft.

She was so caught up in pleasing him she hadn't even realized he'd stopped his movements until he dug his nails into her hips and groaned gutturally. "Ah, fuck. I can't concentrate when you're doing that. I can't think."

"Then don't. Just relax and tell me if I do something wrong."

"Don't stop, and it won't be wrong."

She smiled at his words, at the idea that simple, boring Anita could be causing a macho man like Zane such gratification as to make him mindless. This might be a sin in some people's eyes—namely her parents'—but she didn't care any longer. She didn't care about anything but feeling him explode into her mouth. Suddenly desperate for just that she increased the pressure of her lips on his cock. Releasing his balls, she slid her hand around to his taut ass and fingered his crack the way he'd done to her the day before. It had felt so amazingly good. The harsh grunt that stole from his lips ensured her he enjoyed the unexpected entry every bit as much as she had.

She buried her fingers into his buttocks and his big body shook. She didn't have to work her mouth up and down his shaft any longer, he was doing all the work for her. Her lips slid repeatedly over his hardened length, her tongue coasting over inch after inch of trembling masculinity. He tensed in her mouth, and she gripped his ass hard in her palms as her own body grew tight with the realization he was about to climax.

He thrust between her lips one last time and then with a feral cry called out her name. As his hot come filled her mouth and coated her throat she realized she'd been wrong with her brazen words. She hadn't engrained herself in his memory by taking him so boldly. No, what she'd done was chisel him into her own mind. And how on earth was she ever going to get him out?

\* \* \* \* \*

Zane wasn't exactly sure how Anita ended up staying the night again. The day just wore on, the storm grew worse, and somewhere along the way they'd reached the conclusion it wasn't safe for her to drive on the washed out mountain roads. That she probably just better stay right where she was. Truth be told, he wouldn't have a single complaint if she stayed where she was until he had to go to work Monday morning.

He gazed down at her, sprawled out like a warm, contented kitten on top of him. Her cheek rested on his chest and though she'd been quiet for nearly ten minutes, he knew she wasn't asleep. More likely contemplating how her Friday night appointment had turned into a weekend affair. And it was an affair. Maybe not one based on love, but there were definitely some emotions involved to have him aching to kiss her at every turn, not to mention sharing his bed with her two nights in a row.

"Tell me something about you," he uttered softly.

Anita lifted her head and stared at him, clearly shocked that someone who'd pointedly told her he didn't talk about his personal life would have the audacity to ask about hers.

Fine lines crinkled across her forehead. "Like what?"

Wasn't that a good question? It'd been a damned long time since he'd made small talk with a woman. Longer still, since he'd actually wanted to hear that woman's side of the conversation. He shrugged. "Whatever you want, I guess."

"There's really not much to tell."

"Just the typical run-of-the-mill bore, huh?" Zane teased.

She flinched, her eyes flying wide and the freckles on the end of her nose turning deep red. "A bore?" she gasped. "After everything we've done, you think I'm a bore?"

Fuck no, he didn't think her a bore. He thought she was the most exhilarating, albeit impossible to read woman he'd ever met. Like now for example. "That was a joke, Anita. For starters, you're a dominatrix, and that's about as far from ordinary as a girl can get. And for finishers, I've gotten to know you quite intimately and even if it weren't for your career choice, you'd still be exciting as hell."

Her skepticism faded and she eyed him intently, as if she was almost afraid to believe him. "You really think so?"

"What do you mean, do I really think so? Didn't you see the excitement in my eyes back at the lake this afternoon?"

Laughter filled her gaze and she giggled like the schoolgirl he'd first pegged her to be. "It was kind of hard to see your face from my vantage."

He chuckled as well, while his cock stirred to life with the memory of Anita's forceful sucks and the way she'd fondled his ass. That had been a new one for him. New, and worthy of repeating. "All right, you might not have been able to see my face, but you could definitely see how aroused the rest of me was."

"Mmm…" she murmured, licking her lips, "see it and taste it."

Zane's groin tightened at the sight of her little pink tongue flicking over her lips. As appealing as the thought of feeling it on his body again was, he wanted to get a few answers out of her first.

He brought his hand to the back of her head and idly fingered her short, sable curls. The scent of lavender drifted up to him. A smile tugged at his lips at the familiar fragrance even as worry settled in his gut. He shouldn't like the scent of her so much, shouldn't relish the feel of her small, shapely curves in his arms. Not when he barely knew her and the odds they'd see each other again after this were so slim.

"You're from around here?" he asked, before he could stop himself.

"I live in a tiny little town just outside of Burlington. You know the kind where everyone knows everyone else's business, and your parents watch every move you make whether you're five or twenty-five." Her eyebrows drew together. "Why?"

"What about family?"

She narrowed her gaze. "What about them?"

"I don't know. Do you have any siblings?"

"No, I'm an only child. What about you?"

"I have an older sister. We don't talk much." Not at all since the bitch agreed to handle Trina's side of the divorce. He'd always known those two were too close to be good. He'd been right.

"Jordan's sort of like my sister," Anita said, cutting into his thoughts.

"Your instructor?" Zane asked, more than eager for the distraction.

She frowned back at him. "Huh?"

"Jordan's your instructor, right?"

The frown left her face, but a noticeable level of unease replaced. "Oh, yeah. But she'll always be my friend first."

He wondered over her expression, but thought better than to press her just yet. As long as he kept asking questions she was liable to explain her feelings without further prompting. He returned to his idle play with her hair. "My sister had a girlfriend like that when she was younger. Tonya stayed over so much my parents all but adopted her."

"My parents would disown me if they found out I hang around with Jordan."

"Why's that?" he asked, picking up on the edge to her words.

"My father's a minist—" She stopped short, and gaped at him. Her mouth hung wide open. She looked a lot like the Blue Gill she'd caught this morning.

He stared at her, trying to make sense of her bug-eyed expression. "He's a what?"

Anita closed her mouth and rested her cheek back on his chest. "Nothing. He's nothing. Forget I said anything."

Like hell he would. Not when whatever she'd been about to say was enough to make her hide her expression from him. "No, what were you going to say? He's a minist...?" Zane's hand stilled as the rest of the word came to him and his own mouth nearly flopped open. Instead, he retorted, "Your father's a minister?"

"I didn't say that."

"Yes, you did." Though she clearly hadn't meant to. He caught her chin in his hand and forced her to meet his gaze. She looked mortified. "Tell me, Naughty Nita, if your parents would flip to know Jordan's a dominatrix, how would they react if they found out their little girl followed in her best friend's footsteps?"

She jerked her chin from his grasp defiantly, but the color that flared into her cheeks told him exactly how they would react and more, how she would feel—completely and utterly humiliated. "They wouldn't. They don't care how I make a living."

"I find that damned hard to believe." He found it even harder to believe if she truly was a dominatrix her parents wouldn't have found out about it by now. She'd said herself how small the town was. How everyone knew everyone else's business. How her parents watched her every move regardless of age. If that were the case then her family would know all about her, and her blush spoke volumes to the fact they most certainly did not.

"Do your parents know about you?" he demanded. "Do they know how you get your thrills from beating the shit out of people? How you—"

"Zane!"

She was shaking her finger at him. Too fucking funny. And so not the way a dominatrix should act. "What's the matter, princess?" he asked harshly, attempting to break through what he was convinced was a facade, once and for all. "Can't handle a few questions?"

"Not when they're about my personal life." Anita retracted her finger and pursued her lips. "You didn't want to tell me about yours, and there's no way in hell I'm going to tell you about mine. Now, what do you say, Zane? Are we going to play twenty questions or are we going to fuck?"

Honestly, he'd give up sex for the next month to play twenty questions with her, to find out once and for all the truth behind her fluctuating moods—from schoolgirl sweet to sex goddess sinful. Only she clearly had no intention of answering his questions. Least of all about her minister father.

Shit, he'd never seen that one coming. It sure as hell put her blushing side into perspective. As for her other side, the one who tried something a bit more bold each and every time she had her legs wrapped around him—well, her father must've gotten a little too drunk one night and slept with the local vixen.

Anita tipped her head back and trailed her short nails through the light gathering of dark hair on his chest. She rose into a sitting position then straddled his waist with her thighs as she slowly stroked down his muscled flesh. Her small, firm breasts jiggled invitingly just before his eyes.

"So, what's your answer, Mr. Matthews? Do you want to play with Naughty Mistress Nita, or should I chance that storm after all?"

The latter was the better of his two options. The former would only drag him deeper into the spell she was weaving over him. The one that had his mind in a jumble, and his heart experiencing the strangest of sensations. Yet, even as frightening as that spell might be, he wasn't about to let her leave tonight.

As for tomorrow…

She scooted lower on his body, grinding her wet sex against him as she went. Coming to a stop near the top of his thighs, she reached down and palmed his cock. She twined her slender fingers around him, and his semi hard-on turned to an all out erection. She squeezed him in her grip and smiled impishly. "He wants me to stay, Zane. He wants to pay one more visit to Naughty Nita's pussy."

As for tomorrow—well, he'd worry about that in the morning. Tonight he had his own personal mistress to satisfy.

# Chapter Nine

ഇ

Zane woke to sunshine spilling through his bedroom blinds and onto his face. He blinked at the bright light. The storm had gone, he thought groggily, rolling over to pull Anita into his arms, a place where she'd spent a good deal of the night, testing both of their limits and imaginations. He smiled at the memory, at how willing and eager a partner she was regardless if her dominatrix title held true or not. He could get used to a woman like her. Hell, who was he kidding? He already was.

The smile fell from his lips when his arm kept reaching only to come up empty. His gut tightened as realization sank in. More than just the storm had gone since he'd fallen asleep. Anita was nowhere in sight.

The faintest of sounds reached his ears and he lifted his head and looked to the far corner of the bedroom. An adorable brunette's tight, naked backside swayed at him as she shrugged into her slacks. She wasn't gone. Yet. He wasn't foolish enough to believe she hadn't been about to make a clean get away.

Disappointment washed through him. Though she'd made it clear last night she didn't want him to know about her personal life any more than he'd initially wanted to share his, part of him still hoped she'd spend one more day with him. Fuck, he couldn't deny the truth any longer, he wanted her to stay. And not just for the day either. He felt something for her, something new to him, something he'd love to give a shot if only the timing were better.

"Going somewhere?" Zane asked, his voice scratchy.

Anita jerked around hastily, nearly toppling to the floor in the process. She pulled her pants on the remainder of the way as furious crimson streaked her cheeks. Damn, she looked cute when she blushed. Her pert nose was dotted with freckles and her short curls a chaotic mess he was happy to say he'd had everything to do with.

She yanked on her sweater, then again met his gaze. "Uh, yeah…I told Jordan I'd stop by this morning. I don't want her to worry."

Only half believing her, but resigned to the fact he had to let her go, he came up on his elbows. "So, do you have a card? Or is there some way I can call you?"

She tipped her head to the side. "To?"

"To set up another appointment."

"Uh, yeah." She disappeared into the sitting area, then came back with her purse and a business card in her hand. He took the card. It wasn't Anita's, but her friend Jordan's. "Just try the number there. If I'm not available, I'm sure someone will be."

Someone undoubtedly would be, but then it wasn't just someone he wanted. The someone he wanted didn't have a card of her own because she wasn't a dominatrix.

Clinging to that belief, Zane tossed the card to the nightstand and slid from beneath the covers. Anita's eyes flared wide, as he stood naked before her. Her blush fanned ever higher. He would never get over her contrasts, the way she could be so bold one minute and act like a nun straight out of her father's parish the next. Her striking differences were one of the many reasons he found her so unique. Well, that and her ability to stand on her head for countless minutes, while he licked away at her creamy center, but now probably wasn't the best time to think about that.

Needing to touch her one last time, he crossed to her and stroked his thumb over her color-stained cheek. Her unpainted mouth, slightly bruised from the numerous times he'd kissed her during the long night, turned with a frown. Her eyes, twin orbs of glowing gold, seemed to reflect the sadness that ate him.

He'd always been shitty at goodbyes. This one looked to be the shittiest yet.

"What if I don't want just someone, princess?" he asked, longing to ask her to stay, but knowing he couldn't. He had to pack the last chapter of his life away before he could allow another woman into it completely. But there was always the distant future, when all his packing was done. "What if I want you?"

Anita gulped visibly and pulled away from his touch. "Ask for me," she said flatly. "I'm afraid that's about all the advice I can give."

Zane grabbed her arm and yanked her back to him. As much as he'd needed to touch her, he had to taste her one last time all the more. A goodbye kiss if nothing else.

The kiss was wild, as untamed as he felt at this moment, with his heart beating too hard and his body stirring to life with a yearning he knew no woman could ever fulfill the way Anita had. Beyond being wild and blood stirring, it was nowhere near enough. Not where she was concerned.

It was selfish since he couldn't ask her to stay even though he desperately wanted to, but the idea she was about to walk out that door twisted his gut with resentment. He wished to hell she'd never shone up on his bed. No, that wasn't true. If she hadn't shone up he'd still have leftover doubts from Trina's deceit. He was glad Anita had come to him. It just fucking sucked she had to leave so soon.

He skimmed his fingers over her lips one last time, committing their softness along with her upturned nose and wide eyes to memory, then stepped back and smiled. "If you think of any better advice, don't be afraid to call. You have my number."

"Yeah. I'll do that. Thanks." She looked like she wanted to say more, but only a weak smile emerged on her lips before she turned and walked out of his cabin.

* * * * *

The kitchen door banged open, jerking Anita from her quiet revelry, which wasn't that quiet at all considering the T.V. carried on loudly, several feet from where she sat. She wove around a chaotic pile of old newspapers as she made her way to the back entrance. No one came in through the kitchen aside from Jordan. And darned if that wasn't exactly who stood in the kitchen foyer frowning at her.

"What are you doing here?" Anita asked, wondering over her friend's expression. She never frowned, something about premature aging. "Saturday's your busiest day."

Jordan nodded and folded her hand over a hip swathed in a fuchsia mini-skirt that clashed hideously with her bright red hair. "Oh, we're busy all right. As a matter of fact, that's why I drove over here from Burlington. I was hoping you could help me."

She almost snorted. Her? Helping Jordan with work? Not likely. True, the last time she'd helped her friend with work she'd learned a good deal about herself. But she'd also ended up miserable and heartbroken over a man who'd never felt anything for her beyond lust in the first place. "I highly doubt I can help you, but what's the problem?"

"We had a strange call come in. I thought you might know something about it."

A thousand minuscule hairs arced on Anita's neck with her friend's words. The ones she'd feared hearing for over a month now. The ones that had to do directly with the man she'd spent too much time moping over these last weeks. She had to be talking about Zane. Who else would call that she might know something about?

"What?" she asked, struggling to keep the anxiety from her voice. "Why would I know anything about one of your calls?"

"Zane Matthews," Jordan said, tapping a flame red nail against her side. "Ring any bells?"

Anita almost swallowed her tongue as bells rang all through her body, bells of warmth and longing that she'd done her best to deny. She'd even prayed for the desire that consumed her to lessen. But it appeared God wasn't on her side this time around.

"Nope," she squeaked out.

"That appointment I had you cancel for me last month," Jordan prompted.

She nodded mutely, nearly certain she could form words, but not making any promises they wouldn't sound high-pitched. "Oh, right. Him. I forgot his name."

"Interesting, because he sure didn't seem to forget yours."

*"What?"*

Amusement entered her friend's eyes. "He asked to set up an appointment with Naughty Mistress Nita."

"No," Anita gasped, feeling the color leave her face.

"Oh yes, he did, honey," Jordan assured with a wicked smile. "Care to explain?"

Explain? How did she explain something she couldn't begin to understand? She shook her head. "Not really."

"Fine," Jordan agreed much too easily for Anita's liking. "We'll play catch up later, now there's someone who wants to talk to you."

A fresh dose of anxiety stiffened her spine. *"What? Who?"*

The who in question walked through the kitchen door, and Anita didn't have to worry about swallowing her tongue, because her heart stopped altogether. It started again in pounding waves as she stared upon Zane's handsome face. He looked so different. Shaved. His hair trimmed neatly. A polo shirt covered the broad, naked muscles she'd grown accustomed to spending her nights fantasizing about. And yet past those few things, he still looked the same. And oh so good.

She struggled for her voice. "Zane?"

Jordan made a tsking sound. "Forgot his name. Right, honey." She looked from one to the other and her saucy lips tipped wide. "I have to get back to work. You kids enjoy yourselves. Don't do anything I wouldn't do."

"Somehow I don't think that's possible," Zane commented wryly, as the door slammed shut.

Silence fell over the house as he looked back at Anita. They stared at each other, neither saying a word. Finally, she asked, "What are you doing here?"

He shrugged. "Like Jordan said, I want to set up an appointment. When it comes to dominatrices, I can't think of anyone better than you."

Good Lord, the man still thought she was a dominatrix! It was high time she corrected that dirty little lie. "I don't...I mean, I'm not...I don't do that, Zane. I'm not a dominatrix. I made that whole thing up, because...I don't know, just because."

He shrugged again, looking for all the world like she'd confessed she didn't wear black socks on Tuesday, or something equally unimportant. "So, I should probably leave then, huh?"

"Yeah, I guess." But she didn't want him to. And that was really stupid. He wanted the freewheeling woman she'd been that long, steamy weekend at his cabin just over a month before. Only, she wasn't sure she could be that woman. That had been a one-time thing. Her one chance at being naughty. Was it even possible to repeat it?

Zane's voice cut into her thoughts. "Or we could order a pizza, and you could tell me why you made up such a ridiculous and unbelievable lie in the first place."

"Unbelievable?" Anita gasped.

He grinned, his eyes lighting. "You really think I didn't know?"

He had? "Well...yes. What gave it away?"

"At first it was mostly suspicion, but when I called and asked for you and Jordan laughed like I was off my rocker, things were pretty much solidified. No offense to your friend or anything, but you're much too nice to get into that heavy stuff."

He'd suspected all along and he thought she was nice, but then... "Wait a minute, if you know, then why are you here?"

"A date."

*"What?"* She had to be hearing him wrong. Macho men like Zane Matthews did not date conservative, boring women like her. "Didn't you hear me? I'm not a dominatrix. That's what you want, Zane. That's why you set up the appointment with Jordan in the first place. You need someone to control you, someone to punish you."

A deep chuckle rolled from his throat. "That's not even close to what I want, princess. And I never set up that appointment. My buddies paid for you to come to me. You should've figured out that weekend, I've never in my life been the submissive type. I sure as hell don't get turned on by physical abuse."

"But—"

"But nothing. I told you, no matter what you did for a living, you'd still excite me and that I'd still want to be with you. I like you, Anita. I like you a lot. A day hasn't passed that you haven't crossed my mind." He glanced away and drew a noticeably long breath, before again meeting her eyes. "I would have come sooner, but..." He drew another deep breath, and Anita's bewilderment turned to dread.

She balled her hands at her sides, struggling to be patient as she waited for him to continue. What could he possibly be trying to say?

"Remember when you asked me why I wasn't married?" Zane finally asked.

She nodded, remembering that particular incident all too clearly. She'd almost left his cabin that night. There'd been many times since she'd wished that she'd done exactly that. If she'd walked out right then, she'd never have known how incredible it felt to come so completely undone in a man's arms. She'd never have realized the far-reaching limits of her sexuality. Or that when she'd slept wrapped in his embrace, she'd felt secure and at peace enough to sleep the night through for the first time in ages.

"You scared the daylights out of me," she admitted, "it would be hard to forget."

He winced. "I told you I was sorry that night and I meant it. I also told you the answer to your question wasn't important." Apprehension entered his eyes, and she held her breath for his next words. "To me, it wasn't important. But to you it probably would've been."

She let free her breath and frowned. "I don't understand. What are you saying?"

"The truth of the matter is…my divorce was just finalized yesterday. I didn't tell you about it then, because I wasn't ready to talk about it. But more because I thought if you knew the truth, you'd leave."

Anita's jaw flopped open and her eyes widened so far she feared they might never return to their normal position. "Your divorce?" she gasped. "You were married when we…" Oh my gracious!

"Separated, and all but divorced," he clarified. "You have to understand, Anita. I haven't cared about Trina for a long time now. But as I've already told you, I do care about you. And I think we have a shot at something good."

Zane closed the shallow distance between them and cupped the side of her face. His large, lightly callused fingers caressing her cheek felt too amazing to be true. She wanted to be upset with him for keeping something so important from her, but she couldn't be. Not when he was here now, touching her, telling her he cared. And oh, how she cared in return.

"What do you say, princess?" he asked softly. "Do we order pizza in and get to know each other better, or do I leave?"

Pizza. It had been ages since she'd eaten the stuff. Never if the greasy, hand-held variety was what he had in mind. It sounded messy and bad for you, and absolutely wonderful. She allowed the slightest of smiles to curve her lips, while inside her heart warmed with hope. "I say, what do you like on your pizza, baby?"

He pulled his hand away and grabbed her by the shoulders. "Are you sure?"

The light in his deep blue eyes sent her hope soaring. Maybe a man like Zane and a woman like her could date after all. Maybe they could even do a whole lot more than that. And if her parents found out, well she was a big girl now, and if they were going to talk about her anyway, she might as well give them something to talk about.

"I guess that all depends, Mr. Matthews, can I paddle your ass with my oar if the urge strikes me?"

He chuckled heartily, then yanked her tight to him and sought out her mouth with an urgent kiss. "I'm not making any promises, but I'm always open to ideas."

She pulled away on a breathy sigh, her dreams for their future already growing in leaps and bounds. "Then, yeah, I'm sure. And just in case you can't tell for yourself, I care too, Zane. I care about you so much. And I've missed you."

Longing to feel the urgency she tasted in his kiss in the rest of his big body, Anita wrenched his shirt from his jeans, tugged it over his head and tossed it aside. She skimmed her short nails over his mouth-watering muscles, all but salivating at the thought of sucking on the offered up flesh. "Now, until that pizza arrives, how about you help me mess this place up? It doesn't feel quite homey, if you know what I mean?"

Taking her mouth in another needy kiss, Zane popped the button on her slacks and parted the zipper. His fingers skimmed over her newly exposed skin, pushing her pants down and sending blood jetting to her loins.

He drew back, his voice thick with desire. "Yeah, I think I have an idea. And it would be my definite pleasure to get messy with you Naughty Mistress Nita."

"Too bad I'm not naughty."

He raised a dark eyebrow and tore her red silk panties away with a quick rip. Her slacks pooled around her ankles, and he growled his anticipation. "Want to bet?"

# Also by Jodi Lynn Copeland

ဢ

Lions and Tigers and Bears (*Anthology*)
Gold, Frankincense and Myrrh (*Anthology*)
Sons of Solaris: Aries
Sons of Solaris: Taurus
Uncharted Waters
Wild Hearts: One Wild Weekend
Wild Hearts: Wild by Night


# About the Author

ဢ

Jodi Lynn Copeland discovered her love for writing at an early age and soon after that came an even greater love for the hot, steamy romance--some riddled with humor and fun, others shock full of enough dark and emotional baggage to sink a ship. Jodi is married to her real life hero and has more than a dozen children, though only two of them are human and two-legged.

Jodi is an all-around tomboy at heart, which you can often see shades of in her writing. When she isn't writing or spending time at the day job she likes to pretend she really doesn't have, Jodi can be found in the great outdoors, scrapbooking, watching the discovery channel, CSI or 24, or on any given Sunday sacked out on the couch with her family, taking in the latest NASCAR race.

Jodi welcomes comments from readers. You can find her website and email address on her author bio page at www.ellorascave.com

# LESSONS IN LUST MAJOR

*By Tawny Taylor*

೮೦

# Chapter One

## ɛ๑

*Not again! Every time I'm summoned to this room, I end up regretting it for months.* Kate Evans pressed her back against the interior brick wall, knowing the stooped, eighty-something year-old woman standing in front of her was no more pliant. If only Sister Joy Margaret wasn't the principal, the woman who held her future between her bent, arthritic fingers. Then again, next fall, Sister Joy would be retired. Unfortunately, Kate wasn't sure if that was a good thing or not. If nothing else, the little, quick-witted woman was predictably unpredictable.

Which was the main reason for Kate's currently miserable state.

The principal gave her wimple-covered head a firm shake. "Good! I'm glad you came so quickly. Mr. Krupke," her pale gray eyes twinkled as she said his name, "will be here in just a moment, and then we'll go over the details of your trip this weekend. I had to take some money from the art department's budget to send both the instrumental and vocal teachers to the conference, so I'm asking for some small concessions. Sister Mary Martha wasn't happy to lose the money."

*I bet she wasn't. Concessions? How small?* She swallowed a sigh, and turned her head when Sister Joy's office door creaked. But when Lukas Krupke, the school's new band instructor, didn't enter the closet-sized room as she expected, Kate looked at Sister Joy.

"As you know, this is the first year we've been able to afford sending both..."

*Oh, boy, here it comes!* Knowing whatever the principal had to say would be bad, she dug her fingers into the mortar between the bricks behind her back and held on. *Last time this woman did me a favor, I ended up coaching the cheerleading squad for the year.* Teaching girls how to shake their groove thang was definitely not her most developed talent.

Sister Joy glanced up from her desk and smiled. "Mr. Krupke! Please, sit." She motioned toward a chair in front of her metal desk.

*He's here?* Unable to stop herself, she turned to glance at him.

He gave the principal a friendly smile but hung back, standing about a foot away from Kate.

*He sure is.* She sighed.

Sister Joy cleared her throat, an obvious request for Kate's undivided attention.

But it wasn't easy for Kate to tear her gaze away, not with him standing that close. She tried once and failed. He was so much more pleasant to look at than Sister Joy, not that she had anything against older women.

He wasn't what most women would call traffic-stopping gorgeous, but in her book, he came darn close. If she had to label him, she'd call him bookish-handsome, with dark-framed glasses, slightly mussed hair that was a little long for a private high school teacher, and clothes that could probably fit a man almost twice his size—and he wasn't by any stretch of the imagination a small-framed man.

Since his first day, January fifth, exactly thirteen weeks and three days ago, she'd spent many a night trying to imagine what kind of body hid under those saggy pants and oversized sweaters.

He glanced her way, his dark brown eyes—the color of her favorite chocolate—settling upon hers for a moment.

*Yes, handsome! Do you want to tell me something?*

In response to her silent inquiry, he adjusted his tie and turned back to the principal. "You said you needed to speak with me?"

"Yes, Mr. Krupke. Ms. Evans and I were just discussing the Regional Music Educators' Conference this coming weekend."

"Yes." He adjusted his tie again.

"I wanted to send both of you this year, but my funds are limited. I know this is highly unusual, but I wanted to ask if you two could travel together to save a few pennies."

*Travel together?* Her face warmed. Had someone turned up the heat? Sister Joy was always so blasted cold.

As if she'd read Kate's mind, the principal buttoned her cable-knit cardigan sweater over her brown habit. "Now, I'm not asking you to share a room, or anything that atrocious. After all, we are a Catholic institution, and we must live by certain standards…"

*Darn! What a shame.*

"…I'd like you to simply ride together in a small, economy-minded vehicle."

*Also known as my car.* Kate felt herself smiling, even as a case of the nervous jitters overtook her body. Just imagining that bulk of a man crammed into the passenger seat of her subcompact made her tingly all over. He was so…large. And he'd be so…close. For hours.

"Sure. I understand." Lukas gave Kate a nervous glance. "I don't suppose my all-wheel drive truck qualifies as economy-minded. You don't mind driving your car?"

"Oh, no. Not at all. As long as you don't mind cramming yourself into a vehicle the size of a shoebox."

He chuckled and she smiled, enjoying the way the sound bubbled through her body. Their gazes tangled, and Kate held her breath.

"Excellent!" Sister Joy exclaimed, breaking their brief connection. "Then it's settled. Tomorrow morning, you two will depart from here at exactly five A.M. Here are your itineraries. Everything is all set. We'll see you Monday morning."

That afternoon, Kate pulled out an old favorite to teach her beginning choir, *Some Enchanted Evening*. After all, the spring concert was just around the corner. And the theme was *Spring is in the Air.*

After school, she emptied several box-loads of books, papers, and assorted goodies out of her backseat then went to the carwash and spent a bucket of quarters to clean, vacuum, and polish her car, inside and out. Lukas Krupke would spend the weekend in her subcompact. The least she could do was make sure it was clean.

That night, her dreams were filled with the mysterious Lukas, his voice resonating through her mind until she wasn't sure if she was hearing it for real or not. Unfortunately, four A.M. came quickly, ending the erotic dreams. Still half-asleep, she jumped in the shower, washed, spent a few extra minutes on her hair and makeup—after all, Lukas would have to look at her all day, the least she could do was be presentable—made a pot of coffee, and packed her suitcase into her car's trunk. Then off she sped to the school.

Her heart beat at a quick staccato as she turned into the parking lot and parked next to a mammoth SUV. He climbed out and, dressed in his usual sweater and slacks, smiled and waved at her window, then pointed at the rear of her car.

She smiled and nodded, then reached across to crank open the passenger side window. "I had it washed yesterday. I hope it's okay."

He chuckled—that sound again!—and cleared his throat. "It's just fine. I was motioning toward the trunk. Is there room for one suitcase in there?"

Her face instantly flamed. *He wasn't admiring your wash job.* "Oh! Sure!" She hit the trunk button. *What a ditz! He must think I'm an idiot. Relax, or this'll be the weekend from hell! He's a human, just like you...but with a penis... Oh! This isn't helping! He's a music teacher. You have a lot in common. I wonder if he likes kinky sex... Stop it! Forget about the fact that a chuckle from him makes you weak in the knees, or you'll never get through the next three days.*

After stowing his suitcase and locking his truck, he folded his almost seven-foot frame into her tiny car, pushing his seat as far back as he could. It didn't help much. She couldn't help giggling when he sat, his knees poking way up, his head tipped slightly to the side and rubbing against the roof.

He smiled. "Very comfy. It smells nice in here too."

"Thank you. Coffee?" she offered, handing him an extra cup she'd made just in case. She'd stopped yesterday at the coffee shop down the road and ground the beans herself this morning. There was nothing better than fresh-ground coffee early in the morning. "You know, we could take your truck. After all, Sister Joy is paying us mileage, not actual expenses. I'll pay the difference, if there is any."

"No, that's okay. That truck eats gas like the boy's varsity basketball team devours pizza. Gas prices are terrible. We'd pay a small fortune if we took that beast. You don't mind driving, do you?"

"No, not at all." She shifted the car into gear and drove toward the street. "You're perfectly safe. I have a spotless driving record, not a single speeding ticket. And my car just had a tune-up and oil change a couple of days ago."

"Excellent." He sipped the coffee. "Mmmm. Speaking of excellent. This is delicious."

She glanced his way just in time to catch him licking the cream from his upper lip. *Oh, baby. You can lick me anytime!* Her heart rate upped another few hundred beats per minute, and she got warm and tingly all over as she imagined his tongue trailing a path down her neck and between her breasts.

"Red light!" he said.

"Red? Oh!" She slammed on the brakes, and he thrust his arm out in front, catching himself before his chest hit the dash. The car skidded to a stop mere inches from a police car in front of them. "Shit! So much for my perfect driving record."

He laughed, set down the coffee and fastened his seat belt, and she laughed at herself.

"I promise I'll get us there safely. I swear I'm not usually such a nervous wreck. It must be the coffee. I had a whole pot before I left home." She pulled away from the red light, grateful when the policeman in front of them didn't stop her to find out what her problem was. How would she explain that? *Well, officer, this gorgeous hunk of a man here licked his lips so suggestively, and I started to fantasize and then the light turned red...* Nope, she was quite sure that wouldn't fly. Silently, she vowed to keep her eyes on the road. Lukas would be enough of a distraction simply sitting beside her, no need for her to look at him. That would only make things worse.

\* \* \* \* \*

*Utterly adorable, but a hazard on the road.* Lukas Krupke loosened his tie and forced himself to look out the windshield. It was so much nicer to look to his left, at the beautiful woman sitting inches away, but that only made him more uncomfortable—granted in a good way. She had the most beautiful blonde hair, not bottle blonde, soft, natural blonde. Long and silky. He could imagine how soft it would feel falling through his fingers. And her eyes were a gentle baby blue, round and big and open. Her lips were full and begged to be kissed, and her body...lush, full-breasted, feminine. Perfect for loving. His trousers pulled a little snug across the front, and grateful for the fact that she hadn't looked his way in at least an hour, he tugged to adjust them.

She looked, her gaze dropping to his lap then leaping to his face before landing straight ahead again.

*Shit and double shit! What timing.*

She visibly swallowed but didn't say a word.

What could he say? *My cock is wedged in my drawers, bent like my neck. Sorry, just needed to straighten it out for a second*? Instead, he glanced at the road sign and then at the map. "Only another 400 miles to go." *400 miles of torture!*

"Only 400?" She didn't sound any more enthusiastic than he did. "Um, do you need to stop? I think there's a rest stop up ahead a few miles."

*Sure! We can fuck our brains out then hit the road without having to be so damn nervous around each other.* "I could use some...a...stretch. Sure." His stomach growled, reminding him he hadn't eaten breakfast yet. "Could use something to eat, too. It's been a long time since I've been down this way, but if I remember right, the rest stops are spread out along this part of the turnpike."

"That's good to know. I'd better get something to eat, too then… Oh no!"

The alarm in her voice snaked up his spine. "What?" He looked her way.

She pointed at the instrument panel. "The engine light's on. Should I stop, or try to make it to the service center?"

"You better pull off here. I'll check a few things, and if it looks okay, we can continue to the rest stop."

She looked a little panicked as she maneuvered the car onto the shoulder. "I hope it's nothing."

"Me, too." He climbed out, his neck and leg muscles cramping from being in the same position for so long. The brisk wind cut through his thin spring jacket. Getting colder by the second, but grateful for the secondary effects of the chill—at least his pants weren't snug anymore—he limped around to the car's front. "Okay. Pop the hood!" He eyeballed the engine but didn't see anything obviously wrong. Then he walked around to the driver's side.

She peered through the window, her eyes wide as saucers and full of worry. If he could, he'd kiss that worry away, that and the tremble of her lower lip.

"Does it look bad?" she asked after rolling down the window. "I had the car serviced just two days ago. I can't believe this is happening!"

"Can't tell yet. You have a rag or napkin?"

"Let me see." She turned, rummaged through the glove compartment, and handed him a fast food napkin. Her fingers brushed his as he took it, but the touch didn't last nearly long enough. "Will that do?"

*Not at all, but we'll get to the good stuff later.* "Yes, thanks." He checked the oil. Twice. It was bone dry. *Damn!* He slammed the hood closed and folded himself like a contortionist to fit back into the car. "You have no oil."

"How could that be? It was changed."

"They must not have put the oil pan plug in tight enough. At least that's my guess."

"Then we can't drive to the rest stop?"

"Not if you want to have an engine left by the time we get there."

"Oh." She stared straight ahead, and he had to fight the almost irresistible urge to gather her into his arms and kiss away every ounce of worry. She drew in a deep breath, and he watched her chest rise, her breasts becoming more prominent. He spied the faint point of a nipple through her blouse's silky material.

Damn it! Stranded by the side of the road, and all he could think about was the woman's tits! *Get your mind out of the gutter, pal!* "I have a cell phone."

"Oh!" She smiled. "I almost forgot. I have an auto club membership. I've had it for years but never used it." She hesitated, pointing at the glove compartment, which at the moment was behind his bent knees. "Uh...the card's in there."

"No problem." He turned his body toward her and lifted his knees a bit. "I think I can get it." He fumbled with the latch, but it didn't release.

"Sorry. It's a little temperamental." Before he had a chance to reach behind his back, open the door, and climb out of the car and out of her way, she leaned over him.

That was it. Sheer torture!

*God help me! I can't be held responsible for what I'm about to do.* He closed his eyes and inhaled. Damn, she smelled good. Fresh, like spring. Clean and feminine. He felt her breath heating his cheek and reflexively turned his face toward hers. Each heartbeat pounding out a breathless moment in eternity, he leaned forward until he felt the softest touch to his mouth.

"I...uh..." she said, her lips brushing softly over his as she spoke. "I..." She neither pulled away nor deepened the kiss. Instead, she remained very still.

He didn't have the self-control she evidently possessed. The urge was too great for any man to deny. The woman of his dreams, the one he'd been secretly fantasizing about since the day he'd met her, was here, alone, so close he could taste her.

It was now or never, and he liked the sound of *now*.

He captured her head between his hands and pulled her to him, relishing her sweet flavor as his lips and tongue stroked and tasted. She opened her mouth to him, and he dipped his tongue inside. Like honey! He'd never get enough. And as her tongue mated with his, his body erupted into fire, his hands dropped from her face to cup her full breasts.

She moaned into his mouth, and his cock hardened. His balls tightened.

Then she broke the kiss, and as he opened his eyes and gazed into hers, she muttered, "I...I don't know what to say."

He ran his thumb over her puffy lower lip and tried to catch his breath. "Just do me a favor. Don't apologize. I've been waiting a long time to do this, and if you tell me you're sorry, you'll kill me."

Still breathless, dizzy, aching with need, he waited for her response.

"So have I."

His heart jumped as the words wound their way to his foggy brain.

# Chapter Two

ക

*Oh my God! This isn't happening! I'm not sitting in my car making out like one of my students...with Lukas, the man I've dreamed about for months! And I didn't just admit to him I've been waiting for this to happen.* Her breath caught in her throat, and she struggled to release it so she could draw in the next one.

Not that it was against her morals or anything. She was an adult, perfectly capable of making these decisions. And he was too. They'd done nothing wrong. It was simply too good to be true.

With dirty blonde hair, pale eyes that looked plain and cold at times, and about fifty extra pounds, she wasn't anything special to look at. She couldn't remember the last time she'd had sex — at least with a real man, not an imaginary one.

Yet, there she was, staring straight into the heavy-lidded eyes of a man who was clearly turned on.

She figured she had two choices. First, to grab the opportunity and run with it. Enjoy the moment while it lasted, despite the lack of preparation and protection. After all, she hadn't had sex in years. Birth control pills were not on her list of priorities, nor had she bothered to stock her purse with rubbers. Or, second, to hold him at bay until she had time to take care of some delicate matters — and risk him realizing what a mistake it might have been.

Oh, hell! She'd live for the moment! *Okay, stud. I'm game. But I want to see some skin first.* She slipped his tie over his head, gripped the hem of his sweater and yanked it up to his chest, then pulled his tucked button-down shirt out of his pants. One by one, she unfastened the little white buttons on his dress shirt.

Occasionally, she glanced up, noting the strained expression on his face. He didn't stop her. He didn't help her. He just sat, watching and looking a little...pained. "Should I stop?" she asked, after she'd unfastened several.

"Nope."

She continued, only to find a white cotton T-shirt beneath the starched white dress shirt. "Don't you cook with all these clothes on?"

He visibly swallowed as her fingertips slipped under the T-shirt, grazing his stomach. "Sometimes."

What wicked fun! Every little touch, even accidental, seemed to stoke his fire.

"Sometimes, like now?"

"Yeah."

A massive truck roared by, and the tiny car shook, reminding Kate that they were in the wide open. Getting arrested for fucking by the side of the road would be a killer to explain to Sister Joy. *Damn it all! I have to quit, now. While I still can.*

"Maybe we should stop this now, before it goes too far?" She didn't sound convinced, even to herself. And her fingers had ideas all their own. They slid under his T-shirt and tangled in a patch of soft hair on his lower belly.

"Maybe?" His eyes closed.

"I mean, I don't want to." Those rebellious fingers tiptoed a little higher.

He licked his lips, and she licked hers, still tasting him. Her pussy clenched around an aching emptiness.

"Me, neither," he growled.

She forced herself to pull her hand out from under his T-shirt. It nearly killed her to do it. "But what if an Ohio State Trooper knocked on the window just now? Isn't there a law against things like this?"

"I imagine so."

She reluctantly pulled his sweater down. "Sorry, I got a little carried away, I guess."

"No problem." He still didn't open his eyes.

She glanced down, noting a very prominent bulge between his legs. It was even bigger than it had been earlier. Damn, the man was huge everywhere! When she glanced back up, she caught his gaze. He'd seen her staring there! Her face flamed. His reddened.

"I think I'll get out so you can reach that auto club membership card now." The passenger side door opened, and he half-fell outside.

"Are you okay?" She looked through the car, catching another expression of pain as he struggled to straighten his limbs.

"Fine. I'll be fine. Just need a few minutes, that's all."

"Okay." She opened the glove compartment, retrieved the card, and asked for his cell phone, which he produced in a split second before shutting the passenger side door. And after making a quick call, she announced, "A tow truck is on the way. Aren't you getting cold out there?" She shivered as unseasonably cold air blasted through the open window.

"Not yet. If you don't mind, I think I'll stretch a little longer."

She bit back a smile. Either the man was impervious to arctic wind, or he'd been so hot it was taking a long time to cool down.

Or had she scared him so bad he was afraid to get back into the car?

"If you come back in, I promise to behave myself."

He smiled, and for the first time since they'd left the school parking lot, she felt a sense of relief. Straightening his clothes, he strolled around to her window and stooped over. "I trust you. It's me I don't trust."

Her cheeks heated all over again. "Oh."

"I don't know if you knew exactly what you were doing there, but it was absolute torture to not rip that blouse and skirt off of you and…" He shook his head. "I'm sorry. I never talk to women like that. I don't know what's gotten into me. Did you put something in that coffee this morning?"

"No! I mean, not that I know of." She grinned. "But I kind of liked the way you were talking."

He staggered back, almost stepping into a traffic lane then held his hands in the air. "I give up! Here I am trying to be a gentleman, trying like hell to behave myself, and you're making it near impossible."

Another truck rumbled by, blasting its horn, and Lukas jumped closer to the car. "You are nothing like I expected."

She cringed. That didn't sound like a compliment. "Am I that bad?"

"Bad? Hell no! But you may get us thrown in jail for indecent exposure—not that I wouldn't be sitting in jail with the biggest grin on my face. Every guy in the place would be jealous."

"Quit teasing me! Jealous of what?"

"Have you ever looked at yourself in the mirror, Kate? I mean really looked? You're absolutely exquisite."

"Me?" She glanced in the rearview mirror to make sure she was still the same dull Kate she'd always been. Yep. Hadn't changed a bit. Her eyes were still almost too pale to be called blue, her features were still plain and unremarkable, and her hair was still dishpan blonde.

"Yes, you. Don't you see what I see?" He reached through the open window and palmed her cheek. "Your skin is so delicate and fair, like fine china. Your eyes are gentle, the softest shade of blue, and your lips are full. I want to kiss you every time I look at them." He leaned through the window and brushed his mouth over hers, and she sucked in a sharp breath of surprise. "Just like this." He kissed her softly, his mouth tickling hers until she giggled.

111

A horn blared behind them, and he jerked, knocking the back of his head against the top of the window frame. He grimaced, and she reached for him, but he stepped back.

"Sorry to...er, interrupt—you two aren't newlyweds, are ya?" A gray-haired man in a greasy coverall drawled as he stood at the front of the car. "You called for a tow?"

"Yes...I mean...we called for a tow. That was quick," Lukas said, tugging on his sweater.

"Well, you got lucky. I was headed back from a cancelled call when we got yours." He nodded toward the tow truck parked in front of the car. "If you two want to get in there, I'll get you all hooked up. Leave the car in neutral, little lady, if you would."

"Sure." Kate shifted the car into neutral, grabbed her purse and walked to the tow truck, taking a helping hand from Lukas as she climbed into the truck. He scooted in beside her, and his thigh pressed against hers, sending another wave of heat straight between her legs. She held in a sigh and leaned a little to the right when he rested his arm on the seat back. If he wouldn't make love to her, this weekend was bound to be the longest weekend in history!

\* \* \* \* \*

After an hour's ride in a bumpy, bouncy tow truck, sandwiched between the driver who smelled less than pretty, and Lukas, whose nearness made her head swim, she was grateful for the relative spaciousness of the garage's waiting area. She drank a cup of coffee, even though it tasted like road tar, and ate a stale donut for lunch. Lukas kept back, silent and brooding, as if he regretted everything he'd said and done in the car.

The replacement didn't take long, and before she knew it, they were on their way again. The problem was, if the ride earlier had been stressful, now it was nearly unbearable. Willing to risk a ticket, she speeded a bit, anything to get to the hotel and away from this situation—away from Lukas—for a while. It was clear they both needed a little space.

Unfortunately, when they arrived at the hotel, exhausted, starving, and road-weary several hours later, they had to face more bad news.

"I'm sorry, but you were booked together in one room, and there isn't another room available," the perky young woman behind the counter said.

"Are you absolutely positive?" Kate asked, certain she was going to cry if another thing went wrong today. If there'd been a day in her life she would label *the day from hell*, this one had been it. How could she spend the night in the same room—a room with only one bed, to top it off!—with the man who had refused to say a single word to her for the past several hours?

"What about other hotels in the area? There must be some others," Lukas suggested, finally breaking his code of silence.

"Yes!" Kate looked at the woman, not concerned if it was tacky to ask. This was life-or-death. She had to have her own bed tonight. "Can you give us a referral?"

"I'm sorry. But I doubt any of the hotels around here have openings. We have several large conferences in town this weekend. We're all booked up."

"I'm willing to risk it. Can I have a phone book?"

"Sure." The young woman handed her a slim yellow book.

Kate weighed it. Couldn't weigh more than a few ounces. Nothing like the doorstopper of a phone book she had at home. "This is it?"

"We're a small town. There are only four hotels in the area." She smiled at the couple behind Kate and nodded for them to step forward. "Mr. Krupke's all registered. Good luck finding a room, ma'am."

Kate glanced at Lukas. "I'll just write the numbers down and use your phone, if that's okay?"

He nodded. "Absolutely."

"You know," she said, flipping the pages and scribbling down the phone numbers. "If this was all my fault, I'd be apologizing profusely. I can't believe how many things have gone wrong. My car...and then...and now this! I'd swear someone had sabotaged our trip intentionally if I didn't know better."

A little more like himself, he smiled and nodded. "I feel the same way. But at least we've made it here in one piece. We'll find you a room, have some dinner, and by tomorrow, we'll be laughing at today's misfortunes."

"I hope so." She followed him outside, giving him a smile of gratitude as he held the door for her. Such a gentleman. There weren't too many of those around anymore.

Too bad he wouldn't drop the gentleman act just for one night. She'd had a small taste of the other side of Lukas Krupke, and it was heaven.

# Chapter Three

෨

Why would the Regional Music Educators Association choose such a small town for their conference? Who ever heard of a town with only four hotels? Kate smiled at the restaurant's hostess and followed her lead to a cozy table for two in a quiet corner.

"Don't worry about it. I can sleep on the floor for a couple of nights. It won't kill me." Lukas immediately stepped behind her and held her chair.

"Thank you." She smiled at him as he took his own seat. "Someone taught you manners. Doors, chairs, sleeping on the floor. It's very rare these days."

"My mother was a southern belle to the bone. And she insisted every one of her sons learn how to treat women."

"Every one?" she asked, casually, lifting her glass of water. It was hotter than blazes in the hotel's restaurant. She hoped a little ice water would cool her down a bit.

"She had ten. All boys."

She nearly choked on the mouthful of water she'd sipped. She forced it down then gasped. "Ten children? God help her!" Then she imagined herself carrying Lukas's baby, and had to swallow more gulps of cold water.

"We've all grown now, my youngest brother just left home this past fall. He's attending the Naval Academy."

The water wasn't working. She fanned herself with the menu. "Impressive."

"Mother's beside herself with the empty-nest blues. Has been pressuring me for grandchildren since the day Alek left."

"I know exactly what that's like. My mother's been begging for grandchildren, too. I can't tell you how many men she's tried to pair me up with. It seems everyone she knows has a son or a nephew 'just my age'."

He chuckled and nodded, and she sighed at the way laughter played over his features. His eyes sparkled and tiny lines fanned out from their corners. Good God, he was a doll. "I don't think Mother cares who I marry, as long as she gets her grandbaby by summer."

"Well, considering it's spring already, I'd say that's pretty close to impossible, unless you're not telling me something."

"Oh, believe me..." He glanced over Kate's shoulder and his words trailed off.

Damn, that conversation was just getting interesting.

The waitress arrived, smile in place, pencil poised over her order pad. "Hi, I'm Serenity. Are you ready to order?" She took their orders, then, taking Kate's beloved fan away, she hurried off.

Unfortunately, that left Kate sweating like a pig, and it seemed Lukas had lost his train of thought. Or had decided that pursuing it wasn't wise. The sparkle was gone from his eyes, too. A real shame.

"Which workshops are you interested in attending tomorrow morning?" He pulled at the corner of his napkin, and she watched his fingertips pinching and plucking. Immediately, the image of him doing the same to her nipple leapt to mind, only intensifying the torture. "Have you read through the itinerary yet?"

"I have." She fanned herself with her napkin, wishing someone would turn on the air conditioning. Maybe it was only fifty degrees outside, but in here, it had to be at least ninety. Either that, or she was running a fever. Come to think of it, her mind was a little hazy, and her tongue felt a little swollen. Maybe she was getting sick. "I'm thinking about checking out the Using Technology in the Practice Room session."

"I found that one interesting too." He moved his hand, his fingertip rimming his glass.

She stared at the motion, wondering if he knew what he was doing to her. *There are other things I found more interesting, but I won't go there.* "Good," she blabbered, not even sure if she was speaking coherently. "Maybe we can grab some breakfast in the morning and then go to the workshop together."

Serenity returned with their food—at least Lukas stopped stroking his glass! Then again, a part of her wished he resumed the minute the waitress was gone. She set their plates before them then asked if they needed anything else.

"Some air conditioning, if possible," Kate answered quickly.

Serenity eyed her strangely then laughed. Winking her eye, she said, "Oh, yes. It is hot in here. I'll see what I can do." Then she left.

And Kate stared down at her plate, certain that if she stared at Lukas's hunky face for another minute, she'd combust. And how would she handle tonight? With him in the same room? In the dark? What did he sleep in? A pair of pajamas? A pair of sweats, with...*gulp*...no shirt?

Or nothing at all?

*Oh God!*

\* \* \* \* \*

Lukas couldn't stop fiddling with things, his glass, his napkin, his fork. Kate, all flush-faced and pretty, was sitting across from him, in the dim restaurant, just a hint of a coy smile touching her lips. Soft music played. The candlelight from the lone candle on their table flickered, casting warm shadows over her features. The scents of food filled his nostrils.

The whole thing, wrapped up in a cozy little package—woman, music, and atmosphere—was completely romantic, right out of a movie.

It was enough to drive a man crazy.

*Honest, Lord! I'm trying here! You're not making this easy. And, Mother, if I didn't know better, I'd blame this on you!*

He stared down at his plate, hoping the sight of a cheeseburger and fries might calm his racing heart and overactive libido.

Unfortunately, it didn't work. Just the sound of her voice made his cock hard as concrete. This had never happened to him before. He'd never been so overwhelmed by a woman, so overcome by the need to touch her, to kiss her, to listen to her say his name. How would he spend the night in the same room with her and not succumb to temptation? Hell, when she was fully dressed and jabbering about workshops, she was alluring as a siren. What would she do to his self-control when she padded around their hotel room bare-footed in a wispy little nightie?

She sighed, and his body flamed hotter. His balls tightened, and his cock strained in his pants.

*Sweet Jesus, I don't stand a chance. Maybe sleeping in the car would be safer.*

For some reason, the idea of fucking her while they were on a work-sponsored trip, and taking advantage of the lack of accommodations just didn't sit well with him. But would any red-blooded man have the fortitude to stick to his principles in this case? He'd secretly pined for Kate for months! He'd dreamed about her. Fantasized about her. Been mesmerized by her every move. She was so graceful, her every move choreographed.

Yes, he had his chance. But damn if he'd take it, at least if he could help it. This was not the time or the place. He closed his eyes, fortified his resolve, and ate his dinner. It would take every ounce of his self-control, but he'd be a gentleman. That was how he was raised. That was the man he had grown to be. Kate would respect him for it, and he'd respect himself.

"Thank you for sharing your room tonight," she said, her musical voice warming his insides even more. "I really appreciate it."

Now, if only he were blind, deaf, and paralyzed for one night, he might stand a chance of keeping his word.

The rest of dinner, he tried to concentrate on emptying his plate. He hated the fact that he had to be so abrupt when she asked him a question. And he also hated having to avert his gaze. Staring at a half-eaten burger plain stunk, especially with a goddess sitting so close.

A goddess with long, shiny hair and porcelain skin, and a body created for loving…

*I'm doomed!*

The cramped subcompact looked better and better as his strength melted away.

When he'd polished off the last of his burger, and paid the tab, he hazarded a glance her way. She was looking down at her still-full plate, her long eyelashes a dark contrast to her milky skin. A strange mix of childlike wonder and deep thought played over her features, and he ached to ask her what she was thinking about.

Her hands rested in her lap, the only discernible movement the steady rise and fall of her chest as she breathed.

"Are you through with your meal?" His voice broke the silence between them.

"Yes." She looked up and smiled, and he had to remind himself to breathe. Before he had a chance to walk around, she pushed her chair back and stood.

He motioned for her to lead as they left the restaurant, and his gaze, of its own accord, fell to her behind, watching it move under her silky skirt's material. Knowing it had to look bad, him staring at her bottom in the middle of a restaurant, he forced himself to look up as they walked.

The trip up to their room was a silent, tense one. Especially those few moments they were enclosed in the elevator.

Thankfully, it didn't take long for the slug-slow car to climb to the third floor.

And, as he fought with the need to adjust his pants again, he struggled to make the short walk to their room. As they entered, he motioned toward the bathroom. "Do you mind?"

"Oh no, not at all."

He dashed to the relative safety of the tile-walled cubicle, tried to pee—never an easy task with a hard-on—and made a few adjustments to his underwear. Then he washed his hands and exited, spying Kate standing on her toes, trying to reach her suitcase, which he'd temporarily stowed on the top shelf of the metal clothes rack when they'd checked in.

"Here, let me get that." He ran to assist her, reaching over her head to catch the suitcase before it landed square on top of her.

She glanced over her shoulder and smiled. "Thanks." Her teeth bit down on her lower lip.

He clamped his eyelids closed, knowing if he looked at her much longer, all hope of maintaining his self-control would be lost. But as he forced himself to take a couple of long, deep breaths, the sweet, flowery scent of her tickled his nose and filled his mind. And memories of her taste flooded his mouth.

*Just one little kiss. It can't hurt. Like hell, it can't!*

And then, he felt her mouth tentatively rest over his as she stole his choices away. The sound of her breath filled his ears as the light touch intensified into a kiss. It was almost a chaste kiss, gentle, undemanding, not wild or unreserved. But it was enough to drive him over the brink.

*Oh, hell!* He dropped the suitcase on the carpeted floor and lifted both hands to her face. Her hair tangled around his fingers until he closed them into tight fists, capturing the teasing locks. *Stop now while you still can!*

He pulled on her hair, just hard enough to force her head back. Her neck fully exposed, he trailed kisses down its ivory length, inhaling her natural perfume, and the scent of jasmine lingering in her hair. With every kiss, the need winding through his body grew.

She moaned, the sound vibrating just under her sweet skin's surface, and he licked it away then trailed up to her ear, pulling on her hair to urge her to turn her head for him.

"Oh, yes," she moaned. "More. Please." She rested her hands on his chest, and he gasped as the simple touch seemed to sear his skin through his shirt, setting mini-blazes along nerves lying below its surface.

Every one of those nerves led to one place. Between his legs.

As his cock grew harder, his ability to think melted away. Urgent, shaking need took over. He pushed her back until he had her trapped against the wall, and he dropped his hands to her blouse, kneading her full breasts until he couldn't breathe. His mouth claimed hers, kissing her with all the fire and trapped desire he had fought to contain, and she relinquished with a sigh, wrapping her arms around his neck and opening her mouth to his probing tongue.

He needed her pressed closer, ached to feel her body nude against his. Reaching around, he cupped her ass and lifted, and she wrapped her legs around his waist. He broke the kiss only long enough to find the bed and carry her to it.

But as he lowered her down and gazed into her eyes, he regained a fraction of his mind.

"I shouldn't," he whispered between huffing breaths. He ran his palms down his legs, fighting the urge to rip the blouse and skirt from her body.

"Yes, you should." On her back, her hair fanned about her head as she nodded.

"No, this isn't right. Not like this. I'm taking advantage—"

"Taking advantage of what?" She pushed herself up into a semi-reclined position, and her skirt slid up her thighs. "Please. I want you to. I want this. I've wanted it for a long time."

He stared down at the creamy skin slowly revealing itself as she sat. Inch by delectable inch more thigh exposed to him, until he had to bite back a groan of pleasure. His entire body shook with fierce hunger as his mind and will fought for its control.

This was a work trip, a conference paid for by his employers—Catholic nuns. It wasn't the time or place for anything but professional conduct. What if Kate changed her mind afterward? What if she regretted it? She'd hate him for taking advantage of the situation. He couldn't live with that kind of guilt, not when it was avoidable.

He had to stop, no matter how painful it was.

Leaving her on the bed, he ran to the bathroom, cranked on the cold water and jumped in, clothes and all.

# Chapter Four

ᔕ

It was no easy feat falling asleep later that night. Between nagging guilt for Lukas having to sleep in the car, and an overactive-imagination-gone-haywire, thanks to some raging hormones, she tossed and turned for hours. In total, by the time she dragged her tired body out of bed, she'd probably had an hour of sleep, tops.

She showered, fixed her hair, applied a heavier coat of makeup to hide the dark circles, and dressed then headed for the door, intent to hit the hotel's restaurant for a quick bagel or piece of toast. But as she opened it, she halted before running smack dab into Lukas's wide chest—not that she would have minded.

"Hi. Um, I was about to knock." He dropped his raised fist.

"Oh! And I was heading out for something to eat," she stammered, back-stepping into the room. Her gaze wandered over his rumpled form. His hair was slightly messed, like someone had run their fingers through it. His shirt was untucked and wrinkled, revealing a sprinkling of dark hair on his chest, his pants slouchy and creased. He looked utterly delectable. *Now, there's some breakfast!*

"That's fine. I just wanted to shower and clean up before heading to the workshop. You don't mind, do you?"

"Oh, heavens, no! How could I object? You slept in the car. I still can't believe you did that."

He gave her a pained smile—like when someone pays you a compliment on a horrible new haircut—and headed toward the bathroom after swiping his suitcase off the floor. "Not a problem. See you a bit later." He dropped it on the bathroom floor and cranked on the shower.

She stepped out into the hallway, hesitating before shutting the door. "Would you like me to bring something up for you?"

"Oh, no. I'm fine. Thanks. Not much for breakfast. I'll see you at the workshop."

"Okay." As she turned, catching the doorknob and yanking, she caught sight of him shrugging out of his shirt. Damn, that man had some abs! And his arms! Oh...

Unfortunately, the door swung shut much too quickly.

Her conference packet under one arm, her purse slung over her shoulder, she considered coming up with an excuse to re-enter the room but fought the temptation. It would be too obvious. Plus, she assumed he would have closed the bathroom door once she left.

Then again, maybe he hadn't.

A naked Lukas could be waiting inside...and maybe he wanted her to come back in but didn't know how to ask her. Why else would he start undressing with the bathroom door wide open?

Nope. Wishful thinking. That's all it was. He wasn't trying to lure her. Why would he? She'd practically thrown herself at him last night. He knew she was willing.

She went downstairs, her mind playing yesterday's more pleasant events over and over until she was hot from head-to-toe then forced herself to swallow a chewy bagel and coffee before heading to the first workshop. When she found the correct room, Lukas was standing inside the conference room, in the corner, helping himself to a cup of coffee from a silver coffee dispenser.

He smiled at her as she approached him and motioned toward the paper cup in his hand. Immediately, she noticed his tanned, muscular arms. He'd never worn short sleeves before.

"It isn't as good as the stuff you made yesterday, but it's not bad. Would you like a cup?" he asked.

"Sure."

He handed his full cup to her and turned to pour himself another one. And simultaneously they sipped.

A little uncomfortable when their gazes met, and her blood burning her insides, Kate turned her attention to the gathering crowd in the room, noticing something wasn't quite right.

She swallowed a gulp of the hot liquid, thinking aloud, "There aren't any chairs."

"I noticed the same thing."

"And..." She scanned the group again. Some of them were standing in small groups talking among themselves. Others were sitting on mats on the floor. "And...it looks like all of them are paired into couples. Did you notice that too?"

"Yeah."

She set her cup on the table and re-read the room number on her conference itinerary. "This is the right room, isn't it?"

"It has to be. Besides, it can't be a coincidence we both found it. We came separately, unless our itineraries are both wrong."

"Okay." She drank the remaining bit of her coffee and tossed the paper cup in the trash. "We're probably in the right place. Maybe they ran out of chairs...and...all the schools have a male and female music teacher...?" Okay, that didn't sound logical, but what else could she think?

She stuck close to Lukas's side as he wandered to the back of the room, turning when she heard a female clear her throat.

"Hello! And welcome!" A very cute, very young blonde said. She adjusted the belt on her skimpy wraparound dress, which slightly resembled a fancy bathrobe. "I'm Summer. Now if everyone could please have a seat? There are extra mats over here if you need one."

Kate had never seen a workshop taught by a teenager before. Something was wrong. She glanced at Lukas, who was staring straight ahead, his expression the picture of confusion. "This can't be right," she whispered.

"It's in our itinerary." Finally coming back to life, he zigzagged between seated couples, pulled a mat off the stack, and dropped it in an open spot on the floor. "Maybe she's had some plastic surgery to look younger."

"Could it be the wrong hotel? You know, there wasn't a sign outside the conference room. There are usually signs."

"Before we begin," Summer said, "I'd like to see a show of hands. How many here are first-timers to our conference?"

A sprinkling of couples raised their hands, never only one member of a pair.

Another coincidence? How likely was that? Two music instructors in a school or district. One male, one female. And both had never attended an RMEA conference?

Summer smiled at each person who had raised their hands. "Welcome! I'm so blessed you've joined us. Please feel free to ask questions or make comments whenever you like." Then she tugged at her belt, and it untied. "Now, if you would all get undressed, we'll get started with a communication exercise."

*Undressed? Communication?*

Her dress gaped open, and as Kate sat breathless in shock, it slid off Summer's shoulders and fell to the floor.

And she wasn't wearing any underwear. Nor was she carrying around an extra fifty pounds.

*What the hell?* Certain she had stumbled into some reality show, or some kind of joke, she glanced around the room.

Everyone was in some form of undress...except for Lukas and herself. Many were already nude.

*These people don't look like they're joking.*

She glanced at Lukas, and he returned her silent inquiry with a panicked one of his own. "Should we leave?" she whispered.

He visibly swallowed. "Yes!" Standing, he helped her up then picked up both their conference folders before heading for the door. He moved faster than she'd ever seen him move, and she had to practically run to keep up.

But before they made good on their escape, a naked Summer blocked their exit. "Is there a problem?"

Lukas didn't respond.

"I…" Kate's tongue fumbled around in her mouth as she tried to form words. "I…think we're in the wrong room."

"Oh?" Seemingly unaware of her nudity, Summer smiled. "It can be shocking the first time. I understand. But I wish you'd stay. You have no idea what this experience can do for your relationship."

"Relationship?" Kate repeated. "What relationship?"

"It appears you two are having some communication issues. I don't know you, but I sense if you were to strip away your reservations—and that's why we undress—you'd find you both have some things to tell each other."

"That may be true," Kate admitted before she could stop herself. "But we're not here to solve our relationship issues. We're here for the Regional Music Educators' Conference. I don't understand what getting naked has to do with teaching music to schoolchildren."

It was Summer's turn to look shocked. "Schoolchildren?"

"Yes." Kate grabbed her folder out of Lukas's hand. "See? We're here for the Regional Music Educators' Conference. I'm guessing this is not the Using Technology in the Practice Room session?"

"No, not hardly. Oh my! I'm sorry for the mix-up." Summer stepped aside. "But I still think your relationship would be greatly enhanced by my exercises. You're welcome to stay."

"Thanks for the…uh, kind offer, but no." Kate's face heated to the melting point as she followed Lukas out of the room. But before they'd walked to the end of the corridor, she started laughing, and she didn't stop until they reached the hotel room. "I'm sorry, but that was funny. In a crazy way. How did that happen? How did we end up in a room full of naked people? Were we on TV? Or was it a joke?"

"I don't know." Lukas, whose face was as red as hers felt, sat on the bed and flipped open his folder again. "I don't understand this. The information in our packets is correct. We are in the right hotel, on the right date…"

"…with a bunch of naked people getting in touch with each other. Literally."

"Right." The corners of his mouth curled up until a stunning smile touched every one of his features. "You're right, this is funny." He chuckled, the sound bouncing around in her head and playing havoc on her ability to think straight. Clearing his throat, he continued, "But…um, we should find out where the real conference is being held." He flipped open the folder and read through his materials again, and Kate sat on the bed and opened hers as well.

"I don't understand. It's all here. Times, dates, locations. Is this material wrong?"

"We could try calling RME. There's a toll-free number here. Of course, it's Saturday. We may not get anyone."

"Great idea. It's worth a try at least." She watched him reach for the phone, the stretching motion emphasizing the muscles in his arms. *What a sight for sore eyes! You should wear short sleeves more often.*

He dialed and then scowled, silent, evidently listening to a recording.

"Shit." He hung up. "The conference is *next* weekend. It's on the recording."

Kate flipped to the cover page and verified the dates. Her information packet didn't say it was next week. "What's going on here?"

Lukas swept his folder into his hands and scrutinized it as well. His eyebrows huddled low over his eyes, he twisted his mouth until his expression was downright comical. Then a smile slowly crept over his face. "Look at that! Someone did this on purpose."

"Impossible!"

"No, it's true. Look here." He pointed at a sheet of paper.

"What? Where?"

He bent to show her a page. The dates were smudged. "See? Someone tampered with these, changed the dates."

"But why would anyone do that? And who? Certainly, you don't think Sister Joy would."

"I don't know."

"She's a nun! It's impossible. There is no way she'd send us to some naked couple's conference." She giggled, unable to stop herself. Even the thought was ridiculous.

"Well, who else had access to these materials? Sister Joy would have registered us. She would have known the true dates for the conference. Right?"

"Yes…" This was too strange to comprehend, but at the moment, his logic made sense.

"It had to be her."

"If anyone found out, she'd be in a heap of trouble. Why would she take such a chance?"

"I don't know." Lukas closed his folder and tossed it onto the bed. "Although she is retiring at the end of the school year, right?"

"Yes, but…" Did it matter? Only one question hung in her mind. "What do we do now? Go back to the workshop and strip naked?" She chuckled as heat shot to her face. That was such a silly notion. She couldn't do any such thing. For one thing, she didn't look like Summer without clothes.

But seeing Lukas naked might be worth a bit of embarrassment.

She shook her head, unable to believe her own thoughts.

He pulled at his shirt's starched collar. "That...um, conference wasn't for me. I don't undress in public."

"Me either. I won't even wear a bathing suit. But what will we tell Sister Joy?"

His gaze wandered over her body before settling on her face. "You don't think she'll ask, do you?"

It was her turn to yank on her collar. That man's gaze was like lava, leaving a blazing path over her skin as it wandered up and down.

"I...don't know what to think," she stammered. Thinking was becoming very difficult, indeed.

"I can't imagine going back to that room. I've never done anything like that in my life."

*A total shame.* "It would be horrible, wouldn't it? I mean, sitting across from each other, totally nude..." *Horrible, not!* "Staring into each other's eyes. What if they didn't stop there? What if we had to touch each other?" *Oh, God! Or kiss again? Or...oh...*

A sexy flush slipped up his neck and spread over his face. "Yeah, and we had to tell each other our fantasies?" He licked his lips, and she licked hers, remembering how sweet he'd tasted.

*I have only one fantasy and getting naked with you is as close to having it come true as it gets.* She let out a nervous chuckle as she watched him unfasten the top button of his shirt. "What are you doing?"

"Sorry, just loosening the collar. It's hot in here."

*You can say that again!* "We should go home, save her the cost of the hotel."

"But she wants us here. And it leaves records open for scrutiny. What if someone else finds out what she did?"

"You think she wants us here? We don't know that for sure. Maybe someone else did this."

"Who?" He opened another button, and she stared at the bit of chest revealed. He truly had an amazing body, from what little she'd seen.

She'd pay good money to see more.

"We already covered this ground. I don't see how we've missed anything. No one had access to our materials. No one else would dare try to pull something this nuts. Maybe she's had a stroke or something, losing her marbles?"

"I saw no hint of that."

"Me either." He sat on the bed and crossed his arms over his chest. "I say we stay here and make the best of it. It's only one more night."

"Okay."

"How about some TV?" He pulled the tucked tails of his shirt out of his pants and reached for the remote sitting on the nightstand then pushed the button, and the image of two people, naked, sweaty, and kissing flashed over the screen.

"Wrong channel." He punched a button, and a similar scene took its place. An obviously bleached-blonde rode a guy's thick cock, her mouth in a pucker, her eyes closed. "Shit!" He hit the button a third time, and another sex scene took the place of the last one. This time, a woman was taking it doggy style while sucking a second guy's cock. The TV screen went black. "Sorry about that. Damn porn."

"Yeah," she squeaked out between heaving breaths. "Porn." *Turn it back on, please?* She considered jumping in the shower and taking matters into her own hands, but changed her mind when her gaze met his.

He was as hot and ready as she was.

"Maybe we're the ones who are nuts," she whispered.

Without speaking a word, he pushed her onto her back, and she stared at his face, anxious to read every nuance in his expression. "Tell me you want this as much as I do, and that I'm not taking advantage of the situation. Tell me, please." He closed his eyes and pulled in a deep breath through his nose.

"You're not taking advantage, Lukas. I do want this. I've been dreaming of it since the day we first met."

His eyelids lifted and he growled out, "Thank you," before dropping his head to crush her lips with his. The kiss was no-holds-barred, rough, demanding, full of raw emotion. His hands found her breasts, kneading their softness through her blouse.

Returning every thrust of his tongue with one of her own, she arched her back and pressed her breasts higher into the air, wishing her blouse would remove itself from her body. Then, Lukas did it for her, roughly yanking at it until the buttons flew off, scattering through the air.

"Oh, yes!" The sound of material ripping, and buttons popping only amplified the burning hunger building inside her. She reached behind her back to unhook her bra, but he caught her arms and pulled them up, trapping her wrists over her head by one of his large hands. Her pussy throbbed, and she wriggled until one of his thick thighs was trapped between her legs. "More. Please. Oh God."

Lukas licked a blazing trail down her neck, stopping to nibble on each collarbone before biting the flesh of her upper breasts. Then his teeth caught the lace cup of her bra, a thin shield between her sensitized nipples and his mouth, and she groaned in agony.

Only one thought kept pounding through her head, in time with her racing heartbeat. *Fuck me now.* She struggled to free a hand, but he held her wrists in a tight grip. "I want to touch you."

"No." With his free hand, he eased one of her breasts out of her bra. Then he circled her nipple with his tongue before drawing it into his mouth.

"Oh God," she repeated, grinding her pussy onto his leg.

He nipped, and a bolt of pleasure rocketed through her body. "Do you like it when a man takes control in bed?"

Her head was getting all swimmy, and his words bounced around inside for a while before registering. But once they did, she could barely speak. "Yes," was all she could mutter.

"You want to submit to me, don't you?" He freed her other breast from her bra and teased that nipple until she could barely hold back a scream of frustration. Every cell in her body wanted completion.

"Yes," she groaned.

"How much?"

"Can't you tell?"

He released her hands. "Don't move." His hands dropped to her thighs, slowly sliding up, up, up. Her skirt inched up with them until the only thing covering her pussy was her sodden panties. He audibly inhaled. "Mmm. You're so hot and ready for me."

Her eyes half-open, she tightened her stomach, tipping her hips up and dropped her legs open. "Touch me."

"Now, you're hardly in a position to make demands."

She opened her eyes, which she hadn't realized she had fully closed, and started to sit up, but he stopped her with a scowl.

"You want to please me, don't you?"

"You're driving me crazy." She lifted her knees and drew them together.

"Uh uh!" He caught her legs and pulled them apart, and her pussy clenched and unclenched at the gentle force. "I like you just like this." A fingertip teased her pussy through her thin panties, and she moaned. "Yes, this is much better."

Her hands still overhead, she fisted the bedding as he gripped her panties in his hands and ripped them apart. Rough but gentle. Demanding but giving.

She'd never had a lover like Lukas. Breathless, her lungs refusing to allow air into them, she waited for his next touch.

He parted her labia and tongued her clit, and her entire body shook. When he pushed one then two fingers into her empty pussy, she cried out in gratitude. Each swipe of his tongue and each thrust of his fingers sent more lava through her veins as her body soared toward climax.

And then it was there, the flush of impending climax, and she gasped.

He stopped just before she reached the crest, and she moaned. Her body instantly slackened. "Not yet. You can't come yet."

"You're torturing me." She opened her eyes, catching his gaze as he stood up and started to remove his clothes.

When she started to move, her hands itching to run over the flat planes and bulges of his chest and arms, he shook his head.

"Don't move. Stay exactly as you are. I love looking at your pussy. It's so sweet, so beautiful, wet and tight." He gave her a wicked smile. "I want you to touch yourself as you watch me undress."

Touch herself? She'd never done that in front of anyone! It was too embarrassing. "I can't."

"You can." He dropped his pants, revealing a pair of snug black athletic boxers. If the bulge front and center was any indication, he had a huge cock.

He pulled the boxers down and smiled.

Yes, it was huge, long and thick...and completely erect. Much bigger than both men she'd slept with in the past. She swallowed a gasp.

That would not fit inside her, would it? Her pussy ached to be filled, but with that...? "Oh, my...!"

"Don't be afraid. I promise I'll go nice and slow. Trust me."

She nodded.

He gripped his cock in his fist and slowly slid it up to the base and then back down, and his eyelids fluttered over his eyes. "See? Does it turn you on to watch?"

She nodded, then realizing he couldn't see her because his eyes were closed, she half-sighed, half-said, "Yes."

"I want to watch you, too. Touch yourself for me. But keep your eyes open. Don't you dare shut me out."

"How can I do that? I always close my eyes when I…" She didn't finish that statement. She couldn't finish that statement.

He opened his eyes and looked at her with such a hungry expression, it almost made her cower away. "When you do what, love? When you masturbate? Look at me. I'm masturbating for you. Can you see how much I want you? How crazy the sight of your body drives me? Just looking at your ass… And your pussy and tits. They're perfect."

Mesmerized by his heated gaze and the sight of his hand rhythmically caressing his cock, she reached between her legs, dipped a finger into her slit and then traced tight circles over her clit.

His gaze dropped to her hand then met hers again. It was as fierce and raw as any she'd ever seen, and a sense of power spurred her on. Her other hand traveled down, and she pushed two fingers inside her pussy. Her body cried out for more as she pumped her fingers in and out, and she began to tremble.

Her eyelids threatened to fall shut.

"Keep looking at me." His face showed the strain of a man on the verge of losing all control. That tense expression only heightened her body's reaction. "Can you scoot closer to the edge?" He hooked his hands under her knees and pulled as she wriggled, moving her bottom toward the side of the mattress. She stopped when she felt the edge under her ass. "Yes, this is much better." He kneeled and thumbed her clit, drawing slow, lazy circles over it until her pussy was burning with the need to be filled.

She tossed her head from side to side and the sound of her own moans filled her ears. As she lifted her hands to her face, her scent touched her nose and she inhaled deeply. Never had lovemaking been like this.

He pushed her knees apart and back and teased her pussy with the head of his cock. "Have you ever loved a man, Kate?"

"Yes." She gasped as the delicate skin of her perineum stretched to accommodate his wide girth. She wanted him inside, craved to be filled completely.

"Did you give him everything, your mind, body and soul?" His cock slipped inside, but it remained on the very edge, not quite in, but not quite out either.

Her entire being turned into a ball of bound up energy, and she fought to answer him while straining to take more of his length inside. "No. Not everything. Oh, more, please!"

"But you will do that for me. Now. Won't you?"

"Everything? What do you want?"

"I want all of you. Mind, body, and spirit. Will you give that to me?"

"Yes."

He pushed that beautiful cock deep inside, and she screamed.

"Yes!"

# Chapter Five

ॐ

The minute—no, second—he was inside her, he knew there would never be another. In all his years, he'd never felt such an intense connection, and it wasn't limited to a few select body parts.

Unfortunately, the strength of the connection was leaving him almost powerless to hold back, and he bit his lip as he strained not to thrust into her with too much force. While she wasn't exactly a virgin, she was very tight, sheathing his cock in a slick, hot passage. It was damn hard not to come right away and even harder to pull out and put on a rubber.

With that small detail taken care of, he gripped her thighs tighter, his fingers digging into the soft flesh, and relished the feel of his cock sliding almost completely outside her pussy before plunging back inside again. Each time she took him, those walls squeezed him in a perceptible rhythm. He inhaled the scent of her impending climax, which smelled so sweet he was tempted to hyperventilate just to inhale more. His need building with each thrust until he couldn't bear another second of torture, he reached between her legs to pinch her clit.

Immediately she began bucking as her body careened over the edge, taking him with her. He lost complete control, pounding in and out, her pussy milking him until he had not an ounce of strength. Finally sated, spent and dizzy with relief, he withdrew, pulled off the rubber, and discarded it. His legs were rubbery, his whole body weak, as he climbed onto the bed to catch his breath. He gathered her into his arms and held her, his eyes closed, the sounds of their ragged breathing filling the room.

He couldn't help dozing. His body was heavy, his spirit content, his mind groggy. Sharp hunger pains woke him later, and he smiled at the feel of her silky hair spread over his arm and chest. If only he didn't need food! He could stay there, in this bed, with Kate, forever.

He glanced down at her face and kissed her forehead. She looked so sweet when she slept. He hated to wake her.

Carefully, he tried to slide his shoulder and arm out from under her head, but she woke almost instantly.

"Hi, are you hungry?" he asked.

"Was I dreaming, or did we? You know." She pulled her bra and skirt back in place.

"Oh, believe me, that was no dream." He stood up to illustrate, and his cock hardened in response to her open appraisal.

"I see." She giggled. "I wasn't sure if I believed it. I mean, after all this time. Did you know how I felt?"

"Not until this weekend. I wouldn't have dared hope. I've thought about you every day since we met."

"And your students played that joke on you. I felt so bad," she chuckled, the glitter in her eyes belying her words.

"Yeah. At least it was harmless. It only took me an hour or two to clear all that toilet paper off my truck. By the way," he leaned closer, tempted to climb back in bed for a repeat performance, "how did they know what I drove?"

"Well," she fluttered her eyelashes in a false display of innocence. "I didn't tell them. How would I know? We just met."

He knew better than to believe her, but rather than delve too deeply into that subject, he forced himself to find his clothes and dress.

"I have a question for you." She rolled onto her stomach, and he growled at the sight of her firm ass, her skirt so tight it showed her curves to great advantage. Her wavy hair looked so sexy, all tossed and mussed. Her eyes looked as big a as a child's. "What did you mean earlier? About wanting all of me?"

"Isn't it obvious, Kate? I'm in love with you. Have been for months." He waited, his breath stuck between his ribs and his throat, for her to respond. He swore his heart stopped beating, and it wouldn't start again until she told him she loved him too.

Would she? Did she? He knew she wanted him physically.

"I..." She paused, biting a lower lip that trembled just enough to be perceptible. "I never thought in a million years I'd hear you say those words to me."

"Why not? Are you disappointed? Am I moving too fast?"

"Oh, no. Not at all. It's just that. Well." She sat up, and wrapped a sheet around herself, hiding her partly-clad body from him. "Look at me. I'm just an average, everyday girl. A little heavy, even. But you. Look at you! You could have any woman you want. Even Sister Joy gets a little goofy around you."

He felt a blush heat his face. "You're exaggerating."

"Believe me, I'm not. You have the most amazing body I've ever seen. And what you do with it...holy sheesh!"

"But you're the most amazing woman I've ever seen, too." He reached for her, and taking her hand led her toward the bathroom. "Try to see yourself the way I do. Drop the sheet."

Right away her gaze averted from the mirror, and he held her chin and coaxed her to look into the mirror. "You all think you need to be pencil thin to be sexy. Some men don't like women who look like little girls. Look at yourself." He waited for her gaze to settle upon her reflection. "There. See? Your body is all soft lines. Your breasts are full and round, your stomach and legs and arms just right. And your ass. Let me tell you, I've got some plans for that ass."

She giggled, and he smiled at the playful, sexy sound. "You're serious?"

"Absolutely. You're perfect for me. Will you give me the chance to prove how much you mean to me?"

She chuckled again. "It's ironic. That Summer said if we would strip away our inhibitions, we'd both find we have things we've wanted to say to each other. She was right."

"So do you want to go attend one of those naked workshops?"

"Hell no! But after we eat, I'm game for getting naked in the privacy of our room. We have it for another twelve hours or so. Who knows what else we'll find to tell each other."

He pulled her into his arms and hugged her tight, grateful for the series of strange mis-happenings that had brought them together at last. "Thank God for music conferences," he whispered as he kissed her hair.

"And empty oil pans, and booked-up hotels, and porn movies."

Laughing, they ran to the bed, stripped off the rest of their clothes, and hand-in-hand fell to the bed. Food could wait. They'd finally both shed their fears and uncertainties.

Yes, he would always treat Kate like the fine lady she was. But behind closed doors, he'd also enjoy her naughty side. He had a feeling that part of her had just begun to surface.

\* \* \* \* \*

Monday morning, Kate had a heck of a time hiding her goofy grin as she caught sight of Lukas in the hallway outside the band room. After a full weekend spent alternately making love and talking about their feelings for each other and even touching upon their hopes for the future, she felt as giddy as one of her students. She was sure the whole world could see it, too.

Monica, one of her choir students strolled past, just as Kate approached Lukas and gave him a bright smile.

"Hello, Mr. Krupke, Miss Evans," Monica sing-songed, looking a little coy. "Did you enjoy your weekend? How was the conference?"

Kate started to answer, but stopped when realization dawned. She glanced at Lukas, who also seemed to be thinking the same thing.

How would Monica know they'd gone to a conference? They hadn't told anyone but Sister Joy, and she suspected Sister wouldn't tell the students. She never had in the past.

Neither would their replacement, the elderly nun Sister Joy temporarily took out of retirement. Sister Mary Alba could hardly remember her own name, thanks to a moderate case of senility. But she was a whiz at music theory.

"Monica," Lukas asked with a smile. "How did you know we went to a conference this past weekend? It was very nice. Thank you. We both enjoyed it."

"Oh. I..." Monica stammered, her coy expression changing to fear. "I...uh, copied your itineraries for Sister Joy. I'm her student assistant."

"And would you be responsible for making our travel arrangements?" Lukas asked, his smile still in place, which Kate had to give him credit for.

"Well, kind of."

His smile faded for only a brief second before it returned. Actually, it broadened. Then he glanced around, making sure the corridor was clear before saying, "I don't know why you did it or how. But we both thank you."

Monica's mouth gaped open and she staggered backward. "You won't tell Sister, will you? I'm so stupid."

"No, we won't tell, unless you do first," he promised.

"Deal," Monica said, giving them both a leery smile.

The puzzle pieces suddenly fit.

The spring musical auditions had been a couple of months ago, and the students, under Kate's direction, were now in their second month of rehearsals. Monica, a senior, had taken for granted the fact that she would play the lead. Unfortunately, Kate couldn't cast her for the part, and Monica didn't take the news very well that a freshman had been given the lead instead.

But in the past few weeks her formerly negative attitude had taken a noticeable shift. Now Kate knew why.

Monica was Sister Joy's favorite gopher. She would have access to Sister's computer.

Kate swallowed a chuckle. "And next time you don't get the lead in the musical, Monica, I suggest you seek another form of revenge. This one backfired. Big time."

She and Lukas laughed as Monica sprinted away shouting, "Too much information!"

# SEXUAL HEALING

*By Tawny Taylor*

ഔ

# Trademarks Acknowledgement

The author acknowledges the trademarked status and trademark owners of the following wordmarks mentioned in this work of fiction:

Cheez Whiz: Kraft General Foods, Inc.

Corvette: General Motors Corporation

Dippity-Do: Advance Brands, Inc.

Ford Fiesta: Ford Motor Company

Jenny Craig: Jenny Craig, Inc.

Jockey: Jockey International, Inc.

Krispy Kreme: Krispy Kreme Doughnut Corporation

# Chapter One

## ဆာ

"I applaud Dr. Roy's *The Sex Plan*. It proved to deliver immediate detectable health benefits. However, I fear they weren't exactly what the author had originally intended. Poorly researched and packed with ridiculous claims, it reads like a bad infomercial script. I laughed my butt off—literally—proving once again that laughter is the best medicine. Thank you, Doctor Roy. You've saved me hundreds of dollars in *Jenny Craig* meals and low-carb shakes. But seriously, perhaps it's time for the author to quit looking for another way to get cheap thrills and return to practicing real medicine—"

Drunk with amusement as her own words were read back, Lara Woods laughed. "That *Jenny Craig* thing is pretty funny."

Barb, the managing editor of the tri-county's largest circulating newspaper, sighed and shook her head. "You may be known as the harshest book critic in Detroit, but I think you crossed the line with this one." She slid the printed copy of the review across the desk. "I can't believe you talked me into running this. It reads like the ravings of a pissed off ex-girlfriend."

Not missing her editor's dig, Lara shot back, "That's not fair. I was never that man's girlfriend," she said, using two fingers to gesture air quotes as she said the word girlfriend, "let alone ex. We never dated…officially." With a nod of satisfaction, she shut down her laptop, stuffed it into its padded case and zipped it shut. "I wouldn't change a word and you know it. You didn't want to waste your breath trying to convince me, which is perfectly understandable since you'll need it for tonight," she teased.

"As managing editor, you know it's my job to tell you when something isn't fit for print—"

"And as book reviewer it's my job to tell the unsuspecting public what isn't worth shelling out their hard-earned dollars for. That," she pointed at the object of her latest book review, a tasteless nonfiction claiming that sex is basically the fountain of youth, "isn't worth the price of the paper it's printed on. In fact, it's a crying shame that so many perfectly good trees gave their lives to be soiled by this sh—"

"Don't say it."

"Shit. Crap. Poop," she said, each time punctuating the one-word sentence by dropping a book into her canvas bag on the floor. The soft thumps gave the dialogue a nice rhythm. "I've never heard of the publishing house. They must be new but they won't be around long if they keep producing crap like that."

Barb picked up the almost five-hundred-page volume with the tacky cover resembling a poorly designed 1980s romance novel, clinch pose and all, and flipped it over to read the back. "Regardless, as a friend, it's my job to tell you when you're making an ass of yourself. I've failed on both counts."

"Thanks for worrying but I'm willing to take my chances. It's not like I haven't looked like an ass before. Thanks to my big mouth, there isn't a day that goes by that I'm not called an ass by someone. Besides, nobody knows about that little fling but the two of us...assuming Dr. Roy even remembers it. I think he spent the better part of those years in beer-induced oblivion like the rest of us."

"Well, I know about you two."

Lara stood and pushed her chair under her desk, turning to face Barb eye to eye. "And why would you tell anyone?"

"I wouldn't."

"So what's your point?"

"My point is you're asking for trouble. There are probably others who know."

"No one would remember or care. We were in college. Everyone slept with everyone. Who could keep track?"

Barb set the book back on Lara's desk. "Oh, come on! This book can't be that bad. Why are you doing this to the poor unsuspecting doctor? What happened back then is ancient history. Why get revenge after all these years?"

Lara stooped to hook her elbow through her bag's strap then slung her purse over the other shoulder. "I can't believe you think I'm so shallow. I'm not out for revenge."

Barb laughed. "This is the most scathing review I've ever seen you write and you've reviewed stuff worse than this. Look at last week's book. What was the title? There wasn't a single coherent sentence in the whole six hundred pages."

"That book was so bad I had to pity the author." She bent to gather her lunch cooler and computer case then picked up her car keys. "Give me a break. You know I have too much integrity to use my job for revenge. I'm very careful to keep my reviews objective and honest."

"And you honestly don't think the good doctor deserves a little better than this?"

"Hell no! He deserves what I gave him, the little weasel. I swear some people never change. Don't you get it? This book isn't about helping people improve their health. It's a way to get into women's panties." She headed for the office door and pulled on the handle. "Not that I have anything against Adam personally, mind you. We were friends once. And I wish nothing but good things for him. He just wrote a cruddy book."

"Sure," Barb answered in a flat voice.

"I know you don't believe me, but I don't feel like standing here arguing with you. Have a good weekend. See you Monday."

"Are you sure I can't talk you into coming with us tonight?" Barb asked, following her to the door.

"You know how much I hate being the third wheel. Really. I'll be fine. I can handle being alone for a weekend. Have a great time with Frank," she called over her shoulder. Then, succumbing to the temptation to give her friend one final jab before leaving, she added, "And have some sex, for God's sake. You're looking a little weathered these days. According to the nutcase you wrongly titled the *good* doctor—ha, what a joke!—fifteen minutes of oral sex should just about erase those crows feet. I'm sure Frank is willing to oblige. He'd have nothing to lose by trying." She didn't wait for her friend's retort before heading out the door.

There was no doubt what it would be—"Smart ass."

Struggling with a touch of guilt for having nailed Adam to the cross for his sex book—even if it was a piece of crap—she rode the elevator down to the lower level of the parking structure and walked to her car. If there was one thing she didn't like to do, it was to write a really critical review of a book, especially one by someone she'd once considered a friend.

Although they hadn't spoken in over fifteen years, they shared a history she'd never forget. He had been her first, in so many ways. First college crush and first lover.

She could still picture him in her mind's eye, as he had looked so many years ago. And as she'd read his book, she'd wondered if he had changed. Was he still the skinny, awkward guy who seemed uncomfortable in his own skin? Did he still wear those thick glasses that made his eyes look bigger than they really were, like owl eyes? And did he still wear his hair slicked back with Dippity-Do?

She tossed her book bag and computer into the backseat, closed the back door and opened the driver's door, dropping her purse on the empty passenger seat as she settled behind the steering wheel. Just as she was about to shut herself in, an unfamiliar car careened around the corner—a black Corvette—and skidded to a stop directly behind her Ford Fiesta, effectively blocking her from backing out and exiting.

Fearing the worst—perhaps an irate author she'd recently dissed—she quickly slammed the door and locked it. Then she sounded the horn and scrambled for her cell phone. Damn, if it wasn't lost in the deepest recesses of her purse like always. Her hands trembling as she heard a car door slam, she dumped the contents of her purse on the seat.

No sooner did her fingers close around the object of her pursuit than a quick set of raps on the window made her drop it. The phone bounced off the seat and landed with a soft thump on the floor. "Damn it!" she cussed as a second round of knocks made her twist her head to see what kind of psycho had trapped her.

His face looked familiar somehow but she couldn't quite figure out where she knew him from. He was a strikingly handsome guy with dark, curly hair that tended toward the unruly side—much like his driving—dark eyes, a stubbled jaw and lips that curled into a seductive smile.

He looked dangerous, in more than one way.

"Can I help you?" she shouted through the window, hoping this whole thing was a misunderstanding or strange coincidence. Maybe he thought she was somebody else.

"Hi, Lara. Don't you remember me?" He bent to lower his face closer to her window and she studied his features again with a lot of worry and a little curiosity.

Those almost-black eyes looked a little familiar and that smile... Was he someone she'd met at a party recently? The last one she'd attended, a wedding to be specific, she'd overindulged on champagne, something she hadn't done since college...fifteen years ago...

Then it struck her.

"Adam Roy?" she asked, hoping she was wrong, but in awe if she was correct.

His smile broadened.

"Wow, have you've changed." *Holy smoke! He looks so different.*

"Yeppers. It's me, Adam Ant-boy Roy. In the flesh."

*Where are the glasses and greasy hair? And speaking of the flesh, the boy's gained quite a bit of it and from the look of his arms, it's all muscle. Yummy! He's no ant-boy anymore.*

When she didn't respond, he added, "Aren't you gonna get out of that car and give me a proper greeting?"

*Love to give you a proper greeting…or even improper… No, I'd better not.* "Not until I'm sure you're unarmed."

He backed away from the window and raised his hands in the universal sign of surrender. His shoulders looked even broader with his arms held up and out.

She had a weakness for broad-shouldered men. Especially broad-shouldered men with the glimmer of sin in impossibly deep blue eyes, and a body that was clearly capable of carrying out any promise those eyes suggested.

"I'm clean, unless you consider my book a weapon. I have a few in the backseat of my car."

*I can think of a few things you could use as a weapon but a book isn't one of them.* Her face burning, she fanned it with a stray piece of paper she found as she reached to the floor to collect her lost phone. "Well, it is a bit heavy. The book, that is."

He chuckled, the sound bringing a flurry of memories to her mind. Hot and erotic, they weren't the type of memories she hoped to entertain but they were pleasurable.

She shook her head, trying to clear it, and reminded herself that the last thing she needed at the moment was the rekindling of an old flame with a playboy doctor who wrote books touting sex as the cure for every ailment in the medical journals. She could just imagine how many women he'd slept with in the name of research.

Still, she couldn't seem to control her body's natural reaction to his nearness. She squirmed uncomfortably in her seat, her pussy warm and moist, her breathing and heart rate racing out of control.

He took a single step closer again, which did nothing to help her regain her composure. "You always were a straight shooter. I respect that about you. Come out and let's talk. I promise I won't bite."

*You used to, but we probably shouldn't talk about that now.* "How about we go somewhere public? Sorry, but I don't think an abandoned parking garage is the ideal place for a meeting."

"How about a reconciliation?"

"Definitely not that."

"Fair enough. Where do you propose we go?"

"The Coney Island down the street?" she suggested, naming the first place she could think of that was crowded and noisy.

"Perfect. You won't pull a fast one and ditch me, will you?" His eyes glittered playfully as he rested a hand on the roof and leaned so close his breath created little clouds of mist on her window. He was much too close for comfort.

"The way you drive, I'd say that would be impossible."

"Good." He smacked her car roof and she jumped. "I'll see you there." Not waiting for her response, he turned, got in his car and drove away.

Lara took a moment to check her face in the mirror, smooth back her hair and try to gain control of her central nervous system. But even the thought of seeing that gorgeous face again—and that body! Holy smoke!—sent wave after wave of uncomfortable warmth through her.

Sometime between the mid-80s and the present day, the nerd she'd fancied herself in love with had morphed into a stud she could easily lust for.

A stud who'd written a lame book that she'd just ripped apart, she reminded herself.

He had to have an ulterior motive for showing up out of the blue after over fifteen years. Whatever he was up to, she had to be prepared. The good doctor wouldn't get the better of her, no matter how convincing he might be! She'd make sure of it.

# Chapter Two

ഔ

"I take it you didn't care for my book much." Adam pinched his leg, still not convinced he was really sitting across from Lara Woods, the love of his life, sharing a meal, instead of dreaming. He'd fantasized about this day for years, carefully planned his strategy, but had never expected it to come true. He was so close to getting what he wanted now he could hardly contain himself.

Damn, she was hot, even dressed in her conservative work attire, button-up blouse—with too many buttons fastened in his opinion—and loose-fitting trousers. Long chestnut curls cascaded over her shoulders. One hung down her front, the end looping protectively around the swell of her right breast. He didn't remember her hair having those red highlights, but they suited her creamy white skin and fiery personality perfectly.

Petite, soft and curvy, her body was the perfect antithesis to his long limbs and angular build. And her bulldog, tell-it-like-it-is demeanor was a wonderful complement to his more subdued, laid-back one. She was like a blast furnace, instantly billowing out scorching heat while he was a slow-burning wood fire. They both produced warmth, just at different paces.

He couldn't wait for that first venture into the blaze as they made love. Couldn't wait to hear his name uttered on a satisfied sigh. Couldn't wait to hold her as she slept.

To think that all it had taken was forty bucks and ten minutes on the internet to find out where she was living and working, twelve months of writing, and the creation of a new corporation to get there. But every bit of effort, and every penny spent, had been worth it if Lara Woods would be his at last.

She shook her head and set down her fork, leaving the tines resting on the edge of her dessert plate. "No, I'm sorry to say, I didn't like it at all."

"Don't you think your review was a little harsh?"

"No. And I won't apologize for being honest, if that's what you're looking for."

"Actually, I was looking for a retraction," he stated flatly.

She laughed and he savored the sound, even if it was at his expense. He could live the rest of his life listening to that sweet laughter. "You've got to be kidding me."

He intentionally maintained a straight face even though a smile was pulling hard at his cheeks. "No, I'm not. My work was thoroughly researched and I can prove that every claim in the book has a basis in fact." He leaned closer and whispered, "May I ask, how knowledgeable are you on the subject matter?"

She gaped and he couldn't help chuckling. But her surprise was quickly replaced by something far more amusing. He saw the fire blaze in her eyes as she uttered, "My knowledge of the subject matter, as you so politely put it, is none of your concern."

"It is when you publicly denounce mine."

"You put it out for the public to judge. I didn't."

"But you imply you know better." Knowing it would make her squirm a bit, he leaned forward and fixed his gaze on her eyes. "Have you researched the topic thoroughly before stating my claims were ridiculous?"

Her gaze dropped like a hunk of lead, landing on the table. "I did some...reading."

He had her precisely where he needed her. Between a rock and a hard place. A few more nudges and she'd be in his car, riding back to his home. His heart skipped a beat or two at the thought of her in his bed. "How much? I researched the topic for over five years before writing the book," he lied. "I don't suppose you can top that."

"No," she said, inspecting her silverware. "That's not my job." Evidently satisfied the silverware had passed muster, she toyed with the stem of her water glass.

"Your job is to write an honest and fair review, correct?"

"Yes. An honest and fair review." Her gaze still averted, now skipping along the walls, she took a dainty sip of water. As she lowered her glass to the table, her pink tongue darted out to lick away a droplet that had clung to her upper lip.

He caught her hand and held it fast until she finally looked him in the eye. "So if I can prove to you that your review is unfair, then you'd have to retract it. Correct?"

She visibly swallowed, blinked a couple times then said, "That isn't going to happen."

"You won't give me the chance to prove it to you? What are you afraid of," he badgered, knowing full well what those words would do to her.

Defiance flashed in her eyes. She tilted her chin up slightly and pursed her lips. "Nothing."

He mirrored her posture and challenged, "Good. Put me to the test."

She stared at him, her breasts rising and falling quickly, a blaze of frustration and a shadow of indecision battling in her eyes.

He held his breath and waited, knowing that this would be it, the deciding moment. Either he would get the opportunity he'd worked so hard to gain or he would walk away defeated.

Her shoulders dropped a good inch as she conceded, "Fine."

A round of the Hallelujah Chorus played in his head as he struggled not to show her how pleased he was by her decision. He couldn't afford to tip his hand quite yet. "Good." He motioned to the waiter for the check. "Shall we begin tonight or did you have other plans?"

"No, I'm free tonight. What did you have in mind?" She looked a little skittish, not that he could blame her. If she had any notion of what he was thinking, she deserved to be nervous.

"All my...materials...are back at my place. You don't mind going there, do you? It's a short drive."

"Your place?" She eyed him with suspicion and smiled, and he knew he'd been figured out, at least partly. "Exactly what kind of *materials* are we talking about?"

"Well, um, books and articles of course. Oh and...well..."

"Okay. I'm going to be blunt. Please, be honest. Are you trying to pick me up?" She looped her purse strap over her shoulder, running her fingertips along her collarbone.

His eyes followed their path to the long column of her neck then down to the V of ivory skin below it.

He imagined trailing his tongue down that same path, kissing, nibbling. Exposing more skin as he unfastened one button at a time. "What makes you ask that?"

She pulled on her shirt collar, closing the open gap a bit. "Call it woman's intuition."

He forced his eyes up to her face again and cleared the giant lump from his throat. Another had formed in his Jockeys and was making him mighty uncomfortable, not good. Somehow he needed to will that one away before he stood up and showed, not only Lara, but everyone else in the room what he'd been thinking about. "Hey, I'm just trying to prove my book isn't unsubstantiated hype. You agreed to give me a chance to do that much, right?"

"Yes, but I get the sneaking suspicion we're talking about more than reading a few articles." She crossed her arms over her chest, which pushed up her breasts slightly. The top of her shirt gaped open again, giving him a glimpse of the tops of her soft, rounded breasts.

"Sure. But you have an open mind, don't you?"

She narrowed her eyes and licked her lips. "Aha. The truth comes out. How open?"

\* \* \* \* \*

"How about we talk about it on the way to my house? I live only a few blocks away," he said as he stood and dug his keys from his pants pocket. "You can either leave your car here and ride with me or you can follow me. Your choice."

As Lara walked out of the restaurant, she tried to discern whether he was propositioning her or not. All through the meal, she'd tried to read the truth of his intentions in his eyes, but outside of the fact that his gaze tended to settle a little south of her face—something she'd gotten used to, thanks to double-Ds that had appeared overnight at the age of twelve—his words and intentions were ambiguous. She wasn't sure if the subject matter of his book had led her to a wrong conclusion or if her suspicions were right. One thing was for certain—his proposition had struck a curious chord.

If he didn't mean to prove his position by obvious methods, what exactly was he suggesting?

Her face and neck warmed at the thought of a few of the possibilities. Despite the red flashing lights and "danger" beacon sounding in her head, a part of her hoped his methods would lean toward the unconventional side.

It had been eons since she'd last had sex.

"Well, what'll it be?" he asked, stopping next to his racy black Corvette. "Coming with me or following?"

Despite the secret longings his thick arms and broad chest were stirring, she gave him one of her warning glares and said, "You won't try anything funny."

"Absolutely not." He opened the car door for her.

She sank into the seat, looking up. "Why do I feel like an innocent doe being lured into a trap?"

"No offense, Angel," he said, using the pet name he'd given her so many years ago, "but I'd call you anything but innocent." Before she could slug him—and she'd had a nice shot of his more delicate parts—he slammed the car door and rounded the front of the vehicle.

She waited until he'd settled in his seat and started the car before repeating her earlier question. "You never did tell me. How open-minded do I need to be? Am I in for a surprise?"

"I'm sure it's nothing you can't handle."

"That hardly inspires confidence."

"I wasn't trying to gain your confidence. I'm trying to earn your respect. Those are two very different things."

When he shifted his car into first, she braced herself, expecting to be rocketed forward by the powerful engine. She was pleasantly surprised when the vehicle rolled instead. "So you are really serious about this sex-as-a-cure thing? Honestly, when I first read your book, I thought it was some kind of a joke."

He turned his head to face her. "Oh no. It's no joke. I'm very serious about it. The research is there. It's been proven. Sex does provide healing benefits and can slow or reverse aging." He returned his attention to the road as he turned the car down a side street.

She didn't respond, didn't know how to. Other than to restate her position, which she had to admit was based upon limited knowledge, she had nothing left to say. His earnest defense of his work made her second-guess her harsh criticism. Perhaps she should have done some more reading.

They parked in front of a nice colonial. It wasn't overly extravagant or palatial, but it was obviously well cared for. Even in the dim light of dusk, she could see the lawn was lush, clipped short and not a single dandelion spoiled its Kentucky bluegrass perfection. Tidy rows of annuals lined the front walk and both sides of the porch. And more hung in baskets suspended from the porch beams on either side of the front door.

She felt very welcome and safe as she followed him inside.

Right away, she noticed the interior was decorated as traditionally as the outside, which surprised her. She'd expected something more contemporary, and definitely more masculine. "Which way?" she asked, stepping aside to allow him to close the front door. She rubbed her upper arms, chilled slightly.

"Are you cold?" He reached forward, resting one hand on each of her shoulders, and gazed into her eyes, and it seemed like the years since they'd last been together melted away.

She didn't know what to say or do. Confused and befuddled, awash in memories she'd long forgotten, she stood silent, her entire body tingling, and waited for something to happen.

She didn't have long to wait. His tongue darted out, moistening his lips, and hers mirrored its action. He tipped his head and slowly lowered it to kiss her and her eyelids fell closed as expectation buzzed through her system like a bolt of lightning.

His kiss was soft, lazy, undemanding, nothing like what she'd anticipated. It was hardly more than a series of little touches, but the effect was far from insignificant.

The bolt of lightning ignited an inferno that blazed a path from her head to her pussy. She clenched and unclenched the muscles inside and rocked her hips forward and back in the inbred rhythm of lovemaking. She lifted her hands and gripped the rigid flesh of his shoulders while pressing her body firmly against his.

His hands found her hips and pushed her away.

She gasped.

What was she doing?

The kiss broken, her head lost in a haze of desire, she looked into his eyes.

"Easy, Angel. Let's take this slow. Okay?" He traced her lower lip with his thumb.

She briefly considered giving it a little playful bite but decided against it. For one thing, if things got any more heated, she just might lose all common sense and throw herself at him like the shameless hussy she was trying hard not to be. "Take what slow?" she asked, not sure she understood what was happening.

He tipped his head again, this time nibbling one corner of her mouth then the other. "This." He kissed her again. "We want to get the maximum benefit from it, don't we?" His kisses were slowing her thoughts, catching them like hot, sticky tar, making it close to impossible to follow the conversation.

She shook her head to try to clear it. "Huh? Maximum benefit? What are you talking about?"

"The sex."

"Sex? Oh…" As realization dawned, she stepped back and laughed, despite the ticker tape parade going on inside her body. She'd call off the marching bands in a moment. First, she needed to make sure she was understanding him correctly and then she had to punish him a little…for knowing her too well. "You mean we're here to have sex? That's the proof you were suggesting?"

"Of course. What did you think I meant?"

"You little…toad!" She swatted at him and, feigning insult she didn't exactly feel, she stomped past him toward the door. She didn't get more than a couple of steps before he caught her wrist and gave it a sharp yank, pulling her back into his arms.

"Don't pretend you didn't know what I was getting at here. You're sharper than that. And I don't buy this insulted act either." His grip became more a caress as his hands slid up and over her elbows before climbing higher and resting just below her shoulders. His thumbs drew small circles on the sensitive underside of her upper arms, giving birth to a blanket of goose bumps over her entire upper body.

She shivered.

"Tell me you don't want this, that you haven't been thinking about making love tonight, with me, and I'll take you back to your car and leave you alone for good."

She could hardly say that, at least not without lying. And just the thought of him taking her back to her car and disappearing forever left an ugly, empty spot deep inside.

Egads! How had that happened? How had he already wiggled his way back into her heart?

Or had he never left?

He seemed encouraged by her apparent inability to speak and gently pulled her toward the back of the house, crooning, "Come with me. The bedroom's this way, unless you would rather make love right here on the floor. Or on the couch. Or on the dining room table. Wherever. I'm flexible. Do you like doing it outside? My backyard is private. There are only a few holes in the fence—"

"Wait." She halted in the narrow hallway she assumed led to his bedroom, not sure if she should dash in there...or run away.

"What's wrong, Angel?"

That nickname only confused things. Why did he have to insist on using it?

"I'm not sure about this. What exactly are we doing again?"

He chuckled. "I thought that was obvious."

"It is. But... Oh, I don't know. I'm confused. Why'd you have to come racing into my parking garage—and my life—today?"

He ran his fingers through her hair, tugging just hard enough to feel good. "Because I couldn't stay away another day."

She closed her eyes and concentrated on what his hands were doing. One was still in her hair, pulling her head back, while the other was on her hip and sliding around toward her mound. She was helpless to stop it. "But you waited fifteen years."

"And it was," he rubbed her pussy through her pants and her knees buckled, "pure hell," he whispered. Stopping his

160

intimate caress much too soon, he took her hands in his, pushed open the door with a hip, and led her into the bedroom.

"Are we starting where we left off?" she asked as he led her to the bed then motioned for her to sit. She complied and watched as he kneeled before her and slid first one shoe off her foot then the other.

"Only if you want to." He massaged her right foot and she let out a sigh of contentment.

Damn, that felt good! The parade was continuing in earnest. Horns blaring, confetti flying, crowd cheering. "I'm not sure. It's been a long time. I don't think we know each other anymore."

"That's okay. We can just have sex for now."

"But maybe that's not such a good idea. I have principles, you know. What would people think if they knew I slept with you right after that review was published? I think it might seem—"

He stood and pressed his index finger to her lips. "Shush, Angel. Quit thinking and start feeling. You always did rationalize everything to death. No one will know but you and me." He sat next to her on the bed and slipped off his shoes. "There's no pressure. This doesn't have to be anything more than what you want. In fact, if it makes you feel any better, look at it this way. You agreed to let me prove my research. Let me show you how fantastic you'll look and feel after we've gone a round or two. Then you can write your retraction—"

Those last few sentences grated. The parade inside her body came to a screeching halt. The bandleader dropped his baton. The drums stopped booming. The crowd stopped cheering. "A round or two? And a retraction? First, aren't you making a huge assumption? And second, are you seriously suggesting I have sex with you to prove you're right?"

"Oh no. I'm not making any assumptions."

She laughed. "You're mighty confident."

"I have a right to be." His grin registered a ten on the wicked scale. "So what do you say? Let's fuck so I can prove you're wrong for once and for all." He pulled off both socks, balled them together, and lobbed them into the hamper standing in the corner. "Or are you afraid to find out the truth," he challenged just before lifting his shirt over his head.

Sweet Jesus, he had some tight abs!

Whatever insult she'd intended to hurl his way forgotten, she stammered some incomprehensible gibberish and forced her gaze to the wall.

Who would've guessed a terrible review would have landed her in bed with a hunk?

Would wonders never cease?

# Chapter Three

ରୁ

If tonight was Adam's idea of a seduction, he was damn good at it! Even his not-so-subtle nudges were doing their fair share of damage to her resistance.

No denying it, they were striking her in her softest spot — her pride.

No one would tell her she was afraid of the truth, especially a half-naked man!

She snuck another peek and muttered a few expletives under a sigh. How could she possibly deny herself a little taste of that? She covered her face with her hands and tried like hell to remind herself that sleeping with Mr. Hunkyluscious would be a big mistake.

Since when was she afraid of making mistakes?

She felt his fingers curl around hers just before he pried her hands away from her face.

"What are you doing?" he asked. "Please tell me I'm not that horrible to look at."

"Oh, gosh no. That's not it. You are so…I was just trying…shit, I can't talk."

"Then don't." He pushed on her shoulders, coaxing her to lie back. His mouth found hers, this time claiming it with a lot more urgency. His tongue traced the seam of her lips, begging admission, and she opened to it, savoring his sweet flavor. She inhaled sharply when his hands found her breasts and kneaded them. The scents of man and tangy, masculine cologne teased her nose. The sounds of his quiet moans of contentment quickened her pulse and amplified her longing.

"Oh God," she heard herself say just before she dug her fingernails into his back.

He abruptly pulled away, and she exclaimed, "Oh! I'm so sorry. I didn't mean to scratch you so hard."

"No, that's not why I stopped." He pressed his finger to her neck and glanced at the clock on the nightstand.

"What are you doing?" She struggled to wiggle out from under him but he held her fast by pressing down with his chest and free arm.

Lifting his hand, he held up his index finger and continued staring at the clock. After several seconds had passed, he answered, "Checking your pulse, what else? You need to keep your heart rate at one-fifty if we're going to get optimum results."

"Oh God!" She laughed then quickly sobered herself. "Sorry, I see you're taking this very seriously, but this is just too much. Can't we just enjoy ourselves and let nature take care of itself?"

"Not if you want to follow my plan. It's all about delayed gratification. It's a slow burn, punctuated with short intervals of intense fucking. You use more calories that way."

"Give me a break!"

He frowned. "Not already. We're just getting warmed up."

She chuckled. "I didn't mean that literally."

"That's good because I was getting worried if you did. You really should take better care of yourself."

"I do take good care of myself. I only eat junk food maybe once per week. And I'm down to a quart of ice cream a week. That's real progress."

He shook his head and scowled. "After only a few minutes of kissing, your heart rate soared to the one-fifties. That's completely unacceptable."

"Well gosh!" She pressed her palm to her chest, painfully aware of the quick thump of her heart. "Maybe that's because of other…things."

"What other things?"

Her face flamed. Surely he didn't expect her to spell it out. "You know. Anyway, I think my heart's back to a steady pace. Can we continue now or do you need to double-check my vitals?"

"Hmmm…that might not be a bad idea. I'll be right back." He jumped up and strode purposefully toward the door.

She called out to him as he left the room, "I was only kidding!"

He returned a few seconds later, with a blood pressure cuff and a tray of goodies.

She sat up to get a better look at what he was carrying. "We ate less than an hour ago. You're hungry already?"

"This isn't a snack." He stuffed a thermometer in her mouth then wrapped the Velcro cuff around her upper arm and inflated it.

"Well, then what are you doing with it? What do you have there? Is that…Cheez Whiz?" she asked around the glass thermometer flopping around in her mouth.

"Most women don't get enough calcium." He pulled the thermometer from her mouth, checked it, frowned then stuffed it back in her mouth. "Now shush and hold that thermometer under your tongue. I know your temperature isn't ninety-two." Seeming to be satisfied with her blood pressure, he removed the cuff and dropped it on the tray.

"Okay. But if we aren't going to eat that cheese gunk, then what are we going to do with it?"

This time his grin registered fifteen on the wicked scale. He plucked the thermometer from her mouth for the second time, read it then set it on the tray. "You'll just have to wait and see." He stood, carried the tray to the nightstand and sauntered over to her with the bowl of orange goo in his hand. His gaze honed in on the front of her blouse, which she had the sneaking suspicion was coming off shortly.

She gave him credit for fine motor dexterity as he unfastened each tiny pearl button. They looked miniscule in his fingers as he worked them. His face grew tense as each one opened to reveal more of her torso and her white lace demi bra. As the last button opened and the sides of her shirt parted, he visibly swallowed, blinked a few times and bit his lower lip.

Looked like his heart rate might be a little elevated too.

"Is there a problem?" she asked, feeling a little sense of victory at witnessing the loss of his calm, cool and collected visage.

"Oh…no. Absolutely not." He reached for the bowl of molten cheese product and dipped a finger into it then lifted it to her mouth. "Taste."

She opened her mouth just enough for him to slip his fingertip inside. Her tongue twirled around it as she savored the cheesy flavor, licking it clean. He slowly pulled it out but she didn't cease her oral caressing. Her gaze locked to his face to gauge his reaction, she flicked her tongue over his fingertip. "Yummy!" she said in the lowest, lustiest voice she could muster.

Her efforts were rewarded by a significant color change on his face and neck. His ears became the shade of beets, all in all a welcome effect. Between the hunger she saw in his eyes and the bulge she saw in his pants, her heart was skipping right along at a healthy pace.

He cleared his throat. "My turn." He kneeled on the bed in front of her and gently pushed her backward until she was lying flat on her back again. His nose was a fraction of an inch from hers when he moved the bowl out of the way and reached for the clasp at the front of her bra.

Her breath quickened as the clip gave way and the cups of her bra dropped, exposing her breasts completely. She searched his eyes for a reaction and found a flicker of desire. Once again he dipped his finger into the orange goo, this time using it as a lubricant as he traced slow circles around her right nipple. It was warm...so very warm. She sighed.

Then he lowered his head to lick it off. His tongue teased her nipple until she arched her back to thrust her breasts forward.

She ached for more—more touching, more caresses, more everything. Her heart pounded in her ears, the sound blending with the sighs she could no longer hold back. She raised her hands, letting her fingers tangle in his silky curls as he left one breast in favor of the other one.

Who would've thought processed cheese could be so erotic!

One of his hands slid down her stomach to rest just above her mound. Her hips lifted as her stomach tightened.

"Touch me," she begged on a moan.

He shook his head then smeared more cheese on her breasts. "Not yet."

"If you're thinking I need longer to warm up, let me assure you I'm—"

A quick nip on her neck stole away all thoughts from her mind. Whatever she had been about to say completely forgotten, she growled, "Good God!" Hot and cold at the same time, she shivered.

Her breathing quickened even more as he stopped kissing her neck and trailed kisses lower, between her breasts and down the center of her stomach. Her eyes closed, she felt his fingers work the button on her pants, felt it release then the zipper slide down. "Oh yes!" she said, lifting her hips to allow him to pull her pants down her legs.

Her will lost to the instinct of lovemaking and the hunger burning inside, she bent her knees and parted her legs. But his touch didn't come. Instead, she felt the mattress give on either side of her, as if his weight was pressing around her. Disappointed, aching, she opened her eyes.

He hovered directly over her, his bulk held over her body on thick arms and bent legs. His hands splayed on the mattress on either side of her head. His face was flushed, his hair messed, his chest heaving with every breath. "Damn it," he murmured. "You aren't making this easy."

"Am I supposed to?" She pushed her hips up until her mound pressed against the bulge between his legs.

"It would be appreciated." The muscles in his neck so tense she could see the line of each one, he leaned back again, kneeling between her legs. He looked down, and watching him, she felt her pussy grow wetter in preparation for his touch.

Her eyelids hung heavy over her eyes until they finally closed at the instant he touched her.

That first hesitant touch was agonizingly soft. It teased the sensitive flesh of her inner thighs. She shuddered, unable to hold back her body's reaction. As he explored deeper, his finger dipping between her labia and into her sex, every sensation, every sound and touch and smell seemed to be intensified to almost agonizing levels. They all pummeled her body, setting little earthquakes off inside. She felt like she was coming apart, like she was losing control of everything.

One finger teased her clit while two others thrust deep inside her. The heat of an impending climax coated her skin, starting somewhere deep in her belly and spreading up and out. Gasping, she let herself go.

But then he stopped. "Don't come," he commanded.

Her body rigid as she teetered on the brink of orgasm, she struggled to pull in a deep breath. "What?"

He pressed two fingers to her throat.

"What are you doing?"

"Checking your heart rate."

"Now?"

"Yes, now."

"Oh, for God's sake just let me come." She swiped at his arm, knocking his fingers from her throat.

"No. Not yet." He returned his hand to its position.

She gripped his wrist in her hand and asked, "When?"

"Later. Much, much later." He shook his head. "This isn't good. Nope. Not at all. No wonder you thought my book was garbage." He tsked. "Poor thing."

She clamped her legs closed, sat up, and gave him the nastiest expression she could muster. "This isn't funny."

"I'm not trying to be funny." His expression was as earnest as he words. "This is very serious."

"Tell me about it." Not unaware of her heaving breasts and dripping pussy, she crossed her arms over her chest. "For your information, I'm not having fun here. I don't appreciate being teased."

He grinned. "Now you know how I felt back in college."

She stuck her tongue out. Yes, it was infantile, but so had that jab been.

He laughed and she basked in the warmth of his gaze, in the pleasant feeling his laughter stirred deep inside. "Is there something I can do to make it better?" he asked.

"Yeah, you could get undressed. That would be a step in the right direction."

"Fair enough." He reached for his zipper but stopped before pulling it down. "Would you rather I undress myself or let you have the honor?" he asked in the same carefree tone he might use when asking her what soft drink she preferred.

Evidently, he'd conquered whatever difficulty he'd been experiencing before. He was back to his usual calm and collected demeanor and the red tint in his ears had cooled to a slight pink one.

And she was a pile of quivering mess! That just wasn't fair.

"I think I'll watch," she said, gathering some pillows and fluffing them against the headboard. She leaned against them and prepared herself for the show.

"That's fine. But I want something from you in return."

"I didn't know we were bargaining."

He leaned close, brushing his lips over hers in a soft, teasing kiss and whispered, "Life's one big bargain, isn't it?"

Her breath stuck in her throat, she forced herself to hold his gaze and shrugged. "I suppose. What're your terms? I'm listening."

He backed away. "I want you to tell me your deepest, darkest fantasy while I undress."

"My fantasy? What do you need to know that for? Are you doing research for another book?"

"No, nothing like that. I just want to know."

"Well, what if I don't have a deep, dark fantasy? Maybe I'm not the deep, dark kind at all. Maybe my fantasy is light and shallow instead."

"Whatever it is, I want to hear it."

"I'm not much into fantasies. I prefer reality."

"Bullshit."

"Seriously, I've never been a daydreamer. Heck, I hardly dream at night. I think there's something wrong with me."

He caught her shoulders and looked her straight in the eye. "What are you afraid of?"

She was not particularly fond of that drilling gaze. It was almost…intrusive. She needed to keep some distance, to protect herself. Things were happening so quickly. She wanted it, but she was scared too. Fearful of trusting him, of falling for him and being disappointed again, of being hurt. She dropped her gaze, semi-focusing on the bedding. It had a subtle tone-on-tone thing going on. "I'm not afraid of anything."

He pressed a fingertip to the underside of her chin. "You're hiding."

"Am not."

"Then why won't you look at me."

"I am." She lifted her gaze to his chest. Now, that was something worth staring at! And it was a part of him. She wasn't lying.

"My face. My eyes. Why won't you look me in the eye?"

"Because you're being so…intense."

"Since when does intense intimidate you?"

That was it! Like it or not, she had to meet his gaze now. There was no letting him get away with that little jab. It wasn't true. Intensity did not intimidate her. Not one little, tiny bit. No sirree. In fact, she was the personification of intensity. She lived her life embracing intensity. "It doesn't."

"Now that's better." He released her shoulders and straightened to his full—and quite droolworthy—six-foot-two-inch height and unzipped his pants.

Speaking of drool, she practically drowned in it, knowing exactly what was in store for her. It might have been fifteen years, but there was no forgetting a cock like his. Long, thick and rock-hard at a moment's notice, it was the most glorious equipment she'd ever seen on a man.

He pushed his pants down to his hips.

*Hot diggedy dog! Here we go.*

He stopped. "Tell me your fantasy. Where would you be? What would you do?"

"I can't. This is silly."

Not looking pleased, he sighed and yanked his pants back up and a half-dozen expletives ran through her mind. "Close your eyes."

"What fun is that?" she asked. "I won't be able to see you with my eyes closed."

"Maybe that's a good thing."

Her gaze canvassed what assets it could reach, shoulders, chest, arms. "Oh no, take my word for it, that's not a good thing."

Obviously pleased by her backhanded compliment, he smiled and pushed his pants back down. They hung low over his hips, giving her a nice view of the line of dark hair arrowing down the center of his abs. But his snug black briefs hid all the better parts from view.

Just a tiny swatch of black cotton lay between her eyes and his cock. Feeling herself smiling, she sighed.

That mild reaction was only the start. Other parts of her began rejoicing in their own delightful way, juices dripping, heart beating, palms sweating. It was a flurry of biological celebration. A sensation party.

"Tell me," he repeated, leaning closer until she could feel his breath on her cheek, those delicious abs close enough to lick. She could imagine how they'd taste. He gripped a fistful of her hair at the back of her head and pulled, not too hard but not soft either. The tension tingled on her scalp and another blaze of heat shot straight to her pussy.

His free hand dropped to her breast and squeezed it and she heard the sharp intake of air as she gasped.

This was torture, plain and simple. And she loved it!

Where had he been for the past fifteen years? Why had he waited so long to make his reappearance?

# Chapter Four

**છ**

"I'm waiting," he whispered into her ear.

She shivered as he nipped her earlobe then slipped his tongue inside, tickling her ear until her arm and chest were blanketed in goose bumps.

"Tell me."

"This is silly." She shrugged her shoulder to block his access to her ear.

"No, you're silly. What're you afraid of? I promise I won't put it in my next book."

Despite the fever of unfinished lovemaking threatening to make her go nuts, she laughed. "Well, thank God for that!"

He chuckled, released her breast and scooted off the bed. He yanked his pants up and zipped them.

"Where are you going? I was just teasing about the book thing. Really. I'm sorry."

"I couldn't care less about the book. I'm waiting for you to agree to play along nice."

"Are you serious?"

"Yes."

She sighed and pulled the sheet up, covering her bare torso. "You're a pain in my backside."

Looking quite pleased with himself, he smiled and bent to pick up his shirt off the floor. "Some things never change."

"You have. I mean, on the outside."

"You like?" He struck a pose like a body builder.

It was a very impressive sight.

She felt herself ogling. "Oh yes."

"Then give me a chance here. You're being way too difficult about this. It's not like I'm going to blackmail you."

"Fine."

"Good." He plopped on the bed next to her. "Go ahead, I'm all ears."

"You're not even close to that, but I'll go ahead anyway," she joked. Unable to meet his gaze, she stared straight ahead at the wall. "I always had a fantasy about..." Her pussy tingled and her face warmed. "This is embarrassing."

"Don't be embarrassed. I want to know. There are so many things we don't know about each other."

"I've always wondered what it would be like to be in one of those live peep shows where the guys sit behind a glass window and tell you what to do."

"That's a very sexy fantasy. Have you ever wanted to play it out?"

"No...well, maybe. But not in a real peep show with strangers."

"How about right now? You want to put on a peep show for me? I'm not a stranger."

"That's for sure. But no, I think it'll be disappointing if I actually go through with it," she lied. Just the thought of living out her fantasy with Adam made her hot all over, not that she wasn't already. But another part of her was resistant. "This whole thing is just an experiment to you, a way to prove you're right. Why should I share something so personal as my deepest fantasies with you? I'm nothing more than a lab rat."

"You have a point. Although I have to admit I've never seen such a cute rat before."

She couldn't help giggling. "If you're trying to charm me, you're failing. No woman likes to be compared to a rodent."

"How 'bout a pussycat then? Would you rather I compared you to a kitty?" He stepped toward her, unzipped his pants and pulled them down. With a crooked smile, he kicked them off then pulled off his briefs and tossed them on the floor too.

*Now we're getting somewhere.* Sweet Jesus, his cock was bigger than she remembered. Long, hard and thick. She couldn't help staring as she licked her lips. "This is better. I don't mind the talking, but the time for that is afterward."

"Not if you're trying to produce the optimum effects."

"I'm tired of hearing about optimum effects. I'll give you optimum effects," she teased, reaching forward, wrapping her hand around his cock, and giving it one long stroke. She glanced up at his face to gauge his reaction.

It was as promising as she'd expected. His eyes were closed, his mouth drawn into a narrow line. He growled. The low rumble hummed in her belly producing a chain reaction that ended at her pussy.

She lowered her head and gave the tip of his penis a shy swipe with her tongue. It tasted a little salty from a droplet of pre-come that had gathered on the tip. She opened her mouth to take in more of him. Her tongue swirled around the head, round and round like she was licking a lollipop.

Another moan encouraged her to continue.

She reached for the forgotten bowl of cheese and scooped the now cold and sticky substance out with her fingers and glopped it on the head of his cock. And then with a grin, she went about licking every bit of it away.

As a reward, he uttered moans and groans—and more than a few tantalizing promises along the lines of fucking her into oblivion—until finally he seemed to have had enough. In a stealthy wrestling maneuver, he flipped her onto her back, bent her knees, and pushed them back toward her shoulders.

Her pussy was ready, hot and wet and empty, when his fingertip found her clit. It pressed just hard enough to feel good as it flickered over the sensitive bud, creating an instant flush to her face and chest. She felt the heat climbing higher, felt the tension building inside her belly. And when he stopped, rolled on a condom and pushed that incredible cock inside her, it was all she could do to stop herself from coming.

Her inner walls gripped him firmly as he filled her over and over. With each thrust, she was hurled farther from the world and closer to the oblivion he'd promised her. Her fingernails dug into his back.

Every muscle stiffened, from the top of her head to the soles of her feet as she reached the pinnacle. She screamed, clung to his slick trunk and met his motion thrust for thrust with a tilt of her hips, willing the orgasm to last forever.

He shouted out her name as he found his release and his motions became quicker and jerky as he pumped into her, spilling his seed into the rubber. Within moments, he slowed and pressed a fingertip to her throat.

She opened her eyes and giggled. "How'd I do?"

"An hour and a half? Not bad for your first time. Next time, we'll shoot for longer. Maybe three hours."

"Good God! You're an animal," she said, still giggling like a goofy kid. She hugged him closer, enjoying the feeling of his weight on top of her and the way his damp skin slid over hers. "When's next time?"

"Oh, I don't know." Hugging her tightly, he did a barrel roll onto his back, leaving her on her stomach on top of him. "How about now?"

Her formerly neglected pussy silently rejoiced.

\* \* \* \* \*

The next morning, a groggy, foggy-headed Lara—dressed in Adam's massive T-shirt and nothing else—tried to comprehend the report the scrumptiously nude Adam had slapped in front of her at the breakfast table.

Somehow reading medical statistics took all the sweet out of the OJ and donuts he'd picked up from Krispy Kreme. Not only did the report tell her how many calories she'd burned last night, which only made her feel guilty about the custard-filled pastry she was stuffing in her face, but also statistics on prolactin levels, olfactory nerves, prostaglandin, female hormones, and antibodies. At the end of each paragraph was a list of sources for each statistic. He finished off the report with a list of muscles that would be toned by repeated sexual activity.

She really didn't need to read the last part. She ached in all the right places—thighs, butt, stomach. In fact, she felt as if she'd spent a whole day at the gym.

Yep, she could even admit her mood was lighter, the flowers smelled sweeter, life looked brighter and all that sappy stuff that poets and songwriters tout.

There was just one thing bothering her and it was a biggie.

Last night had been a one-night stand, intended only to prove that sex produced genuine physical benefits—outside of the obvious. Although she'd known that going into it, now she regretted the fact that a more permanent relationship wasn't possible.

Stupid book or not, Adam was a guy she could fall in love with…all over again. If he'd only give her the chance. Last night he pushed the temporary aspect of a one-night stand. He probably had no room in his life for a girlfriend, just like in college.

"I see your point now. You were right." She handed the report back to him and finished her donut. Unable to help herself, she glanced at his butt as he turned away from her to put the juice in the refrigerator. He had one nice ass. Round, firm, muscular. Instantly horny again, she forced herself to look at the clock. It was late. Did he want to get rid of her or would he be game for round number three? "I better get going. I have a lot to do today."

"Like recant a recent review?" He gathered some peaches, berries and a plastic bowl of melon balls into his arms and turned around to face her.

Despite her secret misery, or possibly because of it, she seized the opportunity to get some more sex and delay the inevitable. "Possibly. But before I do that, I think I need to do more research. What do you say? How about some breakfast in bed?" She scooped up another custard-filled donut, ripped it in two and dug out the custard. Her tongue suggestively swirled around her fingertip as she licked it clean.

The result was comical.

His jaw dropped, his eyes bugged and his cock swelled. The fruit he'd been holding in his hands fell to the floor in a pattern of dull thuds, creating a colorful, fresh fruit salad on the linoleum.

That gave her an idea.

Seizing the opportunity, she stripped off her shirt, sauntered toward him and lay smack-dab in the middle of the slippery mess. "Care for some fruit salad?" She scooped up some berries and smeared them over her chest and stomach.

He grinned and licked his lips. "Need my vitamin C. It's vital to a healthy immune system. And blueberries have substances that are known to fight cancer." He hesitated then added, "Be right back."

He turned and ran from the room.

Okay, now she felt silly lying on the linoleum floor amidst squashed melon balls and berries. She combed her fingers through her hair. It was a mess, coated with fruit. What a stupid idea. She sat up and gathered her hair into a ponytail.

He returned, his cock sheathed in latex. "Where are you going?"

"I wasn't sure you were coming back."

"I said I would." He dropped to his knees before her and trailed a finger down the center of her chest. Grinning, he licked it and her gaze locked on his tongue as he flicked it over his fingertip. "Mmmm...I love a good fruit salad."

A huge lump formed in her throat. She swallowed several times and said, "Me too." Following his lead, she ran her hand over the floor, gathering some smashed fruit and smeared it over his hard, lean chest. Then she licked it clean, beginning at the base of his throat, tasting fruit and man.

He kissed and bit her neck and murmured sweet, soothing words into her ear, "That's it, Angel. Yes, you are my special Angel. My one and only." His words warmed her heart as his kisses and soft touches warmed her other parts.

This time, as he pressed her to the floor and leaned down to taste her, she kept her eyes open. Their gazes locked as his tongue traced her slit and his fingers parted her labia, exposing her clit. His tongue danced over it, producing white-hot sparks throughout her body until she couldn't take any more. She needed him inside her, now. She needed him inside her forever. On the verge of screaming with need, she begged. "Make love to me, please."

He sat up, settled on his knees between her legs and with his gaze still focused on hers, drove his cock deep inside.

She sighed with relief, even as the tension coiling through her body tightened. She felt...complete. Warm and loved and whole. Right then. With him.

She wanted to tell him but didn't know how. Instead, she clung to him, nestled her nose into the dip between his neck and shoulder, and took him deep inside. She inhaled slowly, enjoying the way the fruit complemented the just-showered fresh scent of his skin.

They rolled over and over on the floor, slipping and sliding as they made love, their bodies working in complete unity, their hands, mouths, and other parts, both giving and receiving pleasure.

With each beat of her racing heart, she felt their bond strengthening. With each touch she felt her heart filling until she couldn't hold back any longer.

As climax quaked her body, she called out, "I love you!"

He uttered a groan as he climaxed but didn't respond to her proclamation, making her feel like she had so many years ago.

And afterward, he held her close until she squirmed with discomfort from having lain on the hard, cold floor too long.

She wished she hadn't said those words. What had she been thinking? Actually, she hadn't been thinking at all. She'd been carried away by emotions and wishes and dreams, just like she had back then.

Cursing herself for saying those words much too soon, she showered and dressed, the entire time trying to pretend that nothing was bothering her.

The last thing she wanted now was to listen to him give her some inane excuse for not wanting to take things further.

\* \* \* \* \*

He knew he should say something but wasn't sure what. When a guy ignored a woman's confession of love, he knew it was as good as shooting her in the heart.

But he wasn't ready to confess his feelings yet. Yes, they were on the right track. Things were progressing exactly the way he'd hoped, but he didn't want to risk scaring her away.

An intelligent, independent woman, Lara wouldn't appreciate a man who wasn't as independent and strong-willed as she. He'd look like a sneaky weasel if he admitted he'd planned this whole thing to get her back. The timing just wasn't right yet.

But he still couldn't resist saying something. It was her eyes. That darkness, hint of regret. Never did he like to see that, not in those beautiful eyes. Once in a lifetime was enough.

While she showered and dressed, he did the same in the second bathroom then prepared another report about more physical benefits of sex. Her earlier reaction had been priceless, he'd loved it. This second one was sure to earn him a few more eye rolls.

The paper in one hand behind his back, he caught her wrist as she walked toward the door. "Wait."

She looked like she wanted to bolt. Her gaze zigzagged back and forth between his face and the door.

"Before you run away, I want to say something."

He couldn't miss the look of dread on her face.

"If it's about what I said earlier, I didn't mean it. I was just carried away...you know... God, this is embarrassing."

"Don't be embarrassed. I've said some unexpected things in the middle of a climax. It's okay. I promise I won't hold it against you."

She didn't look relieved and he knew why. But at this point there wasn't anything else he could say, outside of "I love you too".

Despite what she thought she wanted, he knew she'd instantly lose all interest in, and respect for him if he told her that now.

"If it makes you feel any better," he added, trying hard not to look like a heartless cad, "I...care a great deal for you too and I respect you. You are an intelligent, beautiful woman and a very giving lover."

Her cheeks stained a charming shade of pink. She stammered, "Thanks, I think." She gripped the doorknob. "Well, you set out to prove your research to me and I have to admit I am impressed..."

He chuckled and the pink stain on her cheeks changed to more of a scarlet. It was a very sexy hue. He wished he could tear off her clothes and make love to her all over again.

She waved her hands in the air. "Give me a break, would ya? This isn't the easiest topic to chitchat about, you know."

"I know." He felt his growing erection pushing at the front of his trousers. It would be visible at any moment...

Her gaze dropped to his groin and her eyebrows lifted.

Yep, she'd seen it. It was impossible for a guy to hide some things.

"Well." She disguised a giggle with a cough behind her cupped hand. "I guess I better get home so I can write that retraction."

"Are you sure you're ready to do that? I mean, to be absolutely certain, you should follow the full regimen. One night…er, and morning, isn't enough proof."

One corner of her mouth twitched, suggesting a smile, but she remained straight-faced. "Ah, the full regimen. Didn't that require at least three two-hour sessions a week?"

Trying to appear sincere, he nodded, "It sure did."

That same corner twitched again. "I see."

Compelled to explain, he added, "Wouldn't you give a diet at least a week or two before making a judgment? It takes time for the full benefits to be seen. Nothing happens overnight."

"You have a point."

*Score!* "So how about next Friday night? We can have dinner first, if you like."

"Dinner sounds nice."

"You still like Thai food? There's a new Thai place opening this week right down the street."

"Yes, I love Thai. What time?"

"How about I pick you up at seven? Will that give you enough time to get home from work, tidy up, whatever you ladies do after working a long day?"

"That's perfect. I'll see you Friday then, for food and sex." She chuckled then pulled open the door. "What I do for my job!"

"Don't forget this." He handed her the report and followed her out to the car.

Her laughter as he drove her back to the restaurant fed his spirit. Next Friday couldn't come soon enough!

# Chapter Five

**ဢ**

Barb's eyebrows rose a quarter inch with every paragraph she read. When she reached the end of the page, she set the paper down and gave Lara one of her patented—and fairly intimidating—"what the hell is going on" glares. When Lara didn't stammer out an explanation, Barb asked, "Do you really want me to print this?"

"Yes." Lara gave her head a decisive nod then inched toward the door, figuring if she left the room quick enough she wouldn't have to say another word.

This was the right thing to do, even if it did jeopardize her reputation for fair and honest reviews. Adam didn't deserve the grilling she'd given him. As she closed her fist around the doorknob, Barb's voice cut through the room, halting her progress. So much for a quick exit.

"Care to explain what this is all about?" Barb said in her don't-give-me-this-bullshit voice. It was not a mere question. It was a demand. For answers.

And based on past experience, Lara knew that voice never went unheeded. Still, she was willing to try sidestepping the issue if possible. It never hurt to try. "I think it's pretty self-explanatory, isn't it?"

"Sit." Barb's prior glare borrowed a little menace from her voice and the end result was both a little amusing and a lot threatening.

Scary, pissed off editor or not, Lara did not follow orders like a dog. She remained standing. "Thanks, but I think I'll stand."

"Suit yourself." Barb read the paper that Lara had given her again then raised her gaze to Lara's face. "What is this?"

"A retraction," Lara stated the obvious matter-of-factly.

"I know that." Barb dropped her palm to her desktop. It landed with a hollow slap. "But what's this all about? You know I didn't want to print that review of Dr. Roy's book. I went out on a limb. Took hell from Max, my boss. You remember him? The guy who signs both of our paychecks? The only thing that saved us both from being thrown out of here were the bags of mail we received in response to that review. Evidently Detroit readers love to see one of their own burned at the stake."

"That's not a particularly pleasant fact to learn."

"And now you want me to print this…this sorry attempt at a rebuttal? It doesn't even make any sense. It's vague and illogical."

"But you have to."

"No, I don't have to do anything. You're really pushing here. Pushing me as an editor and as a friend."

"I know I am. And if it helps, I'm sorry. Really. But I did some…research and well…his book has—"

"What kind of research? Give me something here. Some references to cite. Anything substantial. Then I'll print up a real rebuttal, but not this lame crap."

"It's not that easy."

"Why not? Did you leave your notes at home? Misplace them in that mess you call an office? What?" Barb demanded. With each word her voice rose an octave. Another sentence and she'd be shattering crystal.

"Because the research didn't involve reading," Lara blurted.

Barb's eyes about popped out of her head. In fact, they protruded so much, Lara scooped up the garbage can, just in case she had to catch them. Sure, she'd never heard of someone's eyes literally falling out from shock, but at the moment she just felt more secure with something big and hard enough to hide behind, should anything come soaring her way, body parts or not.

"What?" Barb stammered. "What are you trying to tell me?"

"I'm telling you that I tested his theories—" She simultaneously ducked and lifted the can at the same time. She felt a little like a turtle.

"Would you quit that? You should know me well enough by now to know I'm not going to hurt you."

"There was that time when you threw your lunch at me. Remember that time?"

"I had a sandwich. It suffered more from the impact than you did."

Lara stole a quick peek at Barb's face. It was a little red. Her lips looked tight but her eyes seemed to be settling back into her skull. She checked Barb's desk for potential missiles. Fortunately, her desk was clear. Figuring all was safe for now, Lara set the trash can on Barb's desk.

"Mind telling me with whom?" Barb asked.

"Whom what?" Lara asked, having lost track of the conversation.

"With whom did you test the doctor's theories?"

"Oh. That whom." Lara forced herself to look Barb in the eye. She would not be ashamed. She was an adult. She was free to choose who she slept with. She had nothing to apologize for— at least not regarding her choice of bed partners. "With Adam."

"Dr. Adam Roy?" The left corner of Barb's upper lip twitched. That was bad. Very bad. Lara reached for the trash can again.

"Yes." She moved slowly, gathering the metal can to her chest.

Barb crumpled the sheet of paper in her fist and tossed it at Lara's shielded chest. "This conversation is over," she said slowly, deliberately. "Friend or not, you've gone too far this time. You can't write that kind of scathing review, the kind that gets you, the paper, me, a ton of attention, then sleep with the author and write a rebuttal. "

"Okay. I realize I made a mistake by writing that review without doing my homework. And I'm very sorry for that. But my reputation is for honest and fair reviews," she said, emphasizing both the words honest and fair. "I have to give Adam that rebuttal. He deserves it. It's the right thing to do. And if you won't print it, I'll…" she didn't finish the sentence, not sure exactly what kind of threat she was in a position to deliver on. She couldn't fire Barb. She couldn't do anything to the paper. She couldn't take the rebuttal to another paper.

"You'll?" Barb asked, one eyebrow cocked high up on her forehead.

"I'll…quit," she spat out, tossing the only card she had on the table.

Barb stared at her for a long time, probably a few hours, at least. That entire time she stood there, waiting for Barb to speak, Lara's knees knocked together. Sweat trickled down her forehead. Her stomach did a few loops-de-loops "Darn it. Why do you put me in these types of positions?"

"I'm sorry. I really am."

"Me too," Barb murmured.

"What're you sorry for, Barb?" Lara asked, fairly certain some very unpleasant bomb was just about to blow up in her face.

"Sorry to say you don't have to quit."

That wasn't what she'd been expecting to hear. "Thank you!" Lara dropped the trash can on the floor and lunged forward to give her friend a hug. "I swear I won't ever make you print up such scathing—"

Barb held up an index finger, halting Lara's thank-you speech and her intended embrace. "Please, let me finish."

"Oh sure. Whatever you say, Barbie. I promise I'll do it. I owe you big time. You're the best friend and editor in the whole world." Lara straightened back up, figuring lying draped over one's editor's desk was not the place to be during delicate negotiations with said editor.

Barb sighed. "You're not making this easy, Lara."

"What easy?"

"I'm trying to say…I've been your editor and friend for years…but honestly, I think you're burned out, need a change."

"A change? What kind of change?"

Barb sighed again, blinked a couple times. "I'm going to let you go, let you collect some unemployment until you can figure out what you want to do with your life. Maybe it hasn't been clear to you, but it's been clear to me, your heart isn't in this job anymore."

Her stomach in her throat, Lara muttered, "Fine," the turned toward the door.

Barb jumped up and caught Lara's elbow before she rushed from the room. "Lara, don't take this wrong. I still care about you as a friend. What is it about this guy? What made you do it? What happened between you two? Why'd you stay so mad at him for so long?"

Lara shrugged. "Sometimes I ask myself the same questions. He used me, for one. Talked me into sleeping with him, took my innocence then lied to me and dumped me like yesterday's paper. That's what he did. But he's different now and I shouldn't have let my feelings about him affect my judgment like I did. It was wrong. That review might've been honest but it wasn't fair." Yanking her arm free, she left the room, emptied her desk and drove home.

Fired. All because she was trying to do the right thing by writing that rebuttal. Who cared what kind of research she'd done? A rebuttal was a rebuttal.

* * * * *

"So what kind of foreplay do you prefer?"

The calamari that had just started its descent toward Lara's stomach got stuck about halfway to its destination. Between violent coughs, she sputtered, "What?"

"Foreplay? You know, before the main event?" Adam handed her his glass of water. "Um, are you okay? Do you need a drink?"

"Yes," she croaked. "Thanks." She swallowed several gulps of the cool liquid and sighed as she felt the piece of deep fried seafood slide the rest of the way down.

"Better?"

She nodded and pushed her appetizer plate away. It might be a good idea to wait until this subject had been put to rest before she took another bite. "Can I ask for a favor?"

"Sure. Anything." He dug at his escargot with one of those tiny lobster forks.

She wrinkled her nose as she watched him. "That just doesn't look appetizing."

"You'd be surprised. They're very tasty. Want to try one?"

"No thanks. I have a rule against eating anything resembling an insect."

"Actually, snails aren't insects, they're mollusks, a cousin of the oyster. Do you like oysters?"

"Not particularly."

"Well...it couldn't be any more unsettling than the deep fried squid you're eating."

She glanced down at her plate. "I hadn't thought of it that way. I guess because it's cut up, breaded, and called something completely safe sounding, I don't think about what it is. If they just put squid on the menu I probably wouldn't have the stomach for it." Her appetite was fading fast. Whose idea had it been to go for seafood instead of Thai?"

"I see your point. Getting back to our earlier discussion, what's this favor you'd like to ask me? I hope it involves handcuffs, maybe? Or a paddle...or am I dreaming?"

"You're kidding, aren't you?" When he didn't answer, she added, "No, nothing like that. It's a simple request, actually. Next time you're inspired to ask an off-the-wall question like that last one, would you please give me some advance warning, especially if I happen to have food in my throat?"

"Oh. Sure." He slipped a piece of snail into his mouth and chewed.

She leaned forward and asked in a hushed voice, "Why would you ask a question like that at the table anyway? It's not exactly polite dinner talk."

"Well, I figured we were way beyond formal niceties, considering...well, you know." He mouthed, *we had sex*. "I wanted to make sure I had everything I needed for later," he continued, sounding breezy and casual, like he was talking about a completely innocent topic, planning a picnic or something. "Figured I could stop at the store if I missed anything."

"You talk about it like it's a fishing expedition."

"Well, it is an expedition of sorts, but fish? Nah. That's not such a good analogy."

She shook her head and laughed. If nothing else, Adam had sure grown to be a unique individual. She supposed she'd always known he would. But this unique?

"So, are you going to answer?" he prodded.

She had to really think about how to answer his question for a moment. Some things just weren't spoken of. "I guess I like the usual...stuff..." She glanced around the room. The tables were mighty close to each other. No doubt nearby diners were eavesdropping on their conversation. She didn't dare get more specific.

"You're not helping me much here. Should we stop at the local," he coughed to disguise the word "adult" then continued, "bookstore for some edible undies, maybe? Or how about," he looked to and fro, "anal beads," he whispered. "Those are guaranteed to jack up the heart rate a few notches."

She fanned her heated cheeks. "I'm sure they are."

"Do you have a," he leaned forward and whispered, "vibrator? They are always a good choice, though they work a little fast for my taste. You know I prefer to take my time."

"Yes, you sure do." She shifted in her seat. All this talk about sex toys was starting to produce some interesting effects.

He sighed. "You're dodging the question."

"Don't you think we could talk about something else? It's a little crowded in here, if you know what I mean."

He gave the room a casual once-over. "Naw. Those people aren't paying any attention to us. They're involved in conversations of their own. What's wrong? Are you shy?"

"No."

"Are you one of those folks who can do certain things but don't like to talk about them? I mean, if you are, I completely understand. Of course, I have a friend who specializes in—"

"No, before you start analyzing me, Doctor, I'm not repressed or sexually deviant. And I don't need a specialist of any kind, friend or not."

"That's too bad."

"What?"

"The deviant part might have been fun to explore."

She gave him a kick under the table and he yelped.

"Ouch! So, I take it you're into sadism?" he asked, bending to rub his smarting shin.

She laughed, couldn't help it. "No."

He quit rubbing his leg and went back to working on prying those poor snails from their shells. "How about spanking?"

She averted her gaze, unable to watch him eat the slimy innards he'd not-so-gently pried from the shell. "You want me spank you?"

"Oh no. I'd prefer it the other way around. I'd like to spank you. Maybe tie you to the bed…and what do you think of floggers?"

"I don't. Now, stop it," she whispered, spying the waiter coming toward them with their dinner.

Seeming to not understand why she was trying to hush him, he set upon the next victim in the shallow bowl before him and rattled on, "Okay, you say you don't care for floggers, but if you ask me you're in denial—"

"Stop it," she repeated, just before the waiter reached their table. The waiter kept sliding her curious glances as he set the tray of food on a nearby stand, removed their appetizers and placed their main dishes before them. As soon as he was out of earshot, she kicked Adam in the shin again. "See what you've done?"

"What?" He grimaced. "I see—correction, feel—what *you've* done. But me? I'm not clear what I've done to deserve a second kick."

"The waiter was staring at me. Don't tell me you didn't notice. What is with you tonight? You're acting funny."

"You're a beautiful woman. What do you expect? Of course he's going to stare. I would too…if I wasn't already on a date with you," he answered, evading her question.

She poked at her garlic shrimp and pasta. It smelled wonderful. "No waiter has ever stared at me like that before. He heard us—you—talking about…you know."

"He couldn't have. He wasn't close enough to hear us."

"How do you know that? You were too busy mutilating those poor creatures on your plate."

"I knew when he was approaching and lowered my voice appropriately. He couldn't have heard me."

"He heard something." She glanced up. "Maybe they have security cameras above the tables?"

"For what?" He lifted his fork and inspected it. "To make sure no one steals the flatware? This does look like some petty nice stuff."

"You never know."

He tipped his head and studied the ceiling. His eyes widened. "My gosh, I think you're right. I see something."

"Where?"

"There." He pointed up.

She tried to figure out what he was talking about but couldn't. For one thing, the ceiling was painted coal black. And a thick wood beam directly overhead was obscuring her view. "Where?"

"Right there. Can't you see it?"

"The beam must be blocking my view."

"Come over here." He continued to stare straight up.

"Okay, but how about trying to look a little less obvious?"

"Oh yeah. Good idea." He grinned at her as she rounded the table and scooted into the bench beside him. Once she was settled, he lifted an arm and casually draped it over her shoulder.

It felt nice being so close and snuggly. Quite comfy, she reached across the table for her plate and dragged it across the table then asked, "Okay. Where? Don't point. Just tell me. I've always wanted to find those hidden cameras. I've heard they're everywhere—in stores, restaurants—but near impossible to find."

"Does that excite you?"

"I don't know if I'd go that far—"

"Would you like to be secretly filmed? I have a great camcorder at home, a tripod, the whole nine yards."

"No, you goof. I wouldn't. I just want to find the hidden camera here. Now, where is it?"

He sighed and averted his gaze, dropping it to his plate full of steamed fish and vegetables. "I have a confession to make. There isn't one, at least none that I saw. I was just joking."

She gave him a backhand in the gut. "What'd you do that for?"

"Isn't it obvious?" His hand squeezed her shoulder. "You were too far away. I like you closer. You have to admit, this is cozy." He reached across with his other hand, took her fork and stabbed a piece of shrimp. It hovered a couple of inches from her mouth. "Will you let me feed you? Open up and take it all in."

She laughed. "Pervert."

"I'm the pervert? I didn't say anything perverted. You just took it that way."

She opened her mouth and closed her lips over the fork, pulling the piece of shrimp off the tines. It was delicious. "Mmmm…"

"I take it, you approve?" He removed his arm from her shoulder and dropped his hand to her lap. Fortunately, the long tablecloth hid it from view because it no sooner landed than it was venturing down her thigh and under the hem of her skirt.

"What are you doing? You've never acted like this before."

"Serving you." He twirled some noodles on her fork with one hand while the other one inched up the inside of her thigh. "Open wide."

She laughed. "See? You are a pervert."

He waggled his eyebrows. "I don't hear you complaining." A fingertip stroked her pussy through her satin panties.

She bit back a groan and opened both her mouth and legs. His venturesome finger slid up and down her pussy while his other hand lifted her fork. Her eyes closed, she opened her mouth to accept the garlic-laden noodles.

"How is it?" she heard him ask. But with a mouthful of noodles and an empty pussy that was burning to be filled, she was temporarily beyond speech.

His chuckle, which was far from innocent sounding, only intensified her need.

"How is everything here, folks?" she heard the waiter ask. She forced her eyelids to lift and smiled in response to his question.

"Absolutely fantastic," Adam answered. "Don't let the full plate fool you. I'm savoring every morsel."

The waiter seemed pleased, if not a little perplexed. From his perspective, they had to look a strange pair. She could only imagine how flush-faced and out of it she appeared at the moment and Adam hardly looked any better. His ears were the color of the tomato in her tossed salad.

She forced her smile to widen and nodded again, and the waiter hurried to his next table.

"I think he knows what we're doing," she said as she watched his hasty retreat.

"You're paranoid."

"Maybe we should get this wrapped up and take it home."

"No way. I like the atmosphere here. What's the hurry?" His fingertip wiggled under the leg band of her panties.

She shifted her weight, leaning back and tipping her pelvis up to give him better access. Why had she bothered to wear panties at all? At the moment, they were nothing but a nuisance. "You know what the hurry is." Deciding to give him a taste of his own medicine, she dropped her hand to his lap and squeezed the bulge in his trousers.

His response was an indecipherable utterance that hardly registered in her ear. And then he hooked his finger and gave the crotch of her panties a sharp yank.

She heard the sodden material give way and immediately scanned the faces of nearby diners to see if any of them had heard.

If they had, they were hiding their reactions well.

That same naughty finger of his slid up and down her slit. "I could sit here for hours like this," he whispered into her ear.

"I couldn't."

It slipped just inside her pussy and she held in a tortured groan, wrapped her hand around his forearm and dug her nails into it.

"It's healthy to take your time and enjoy a meal. I've read the French are particularly good at that."

"Among other things I'm sure," she muttered just before feeling something tracing the seam of her lips. She opened her mouth, welcoming more seafood and noodles.

He slowly pressed a second finger into her pussy and it was all she could do to stop from howling with frustration. He knew exactly what he was doing and by the varying speed of his strokes, she could tell he was somehow aware of how close she was to climaxing.

Heat traveled through her body in relentless waves. Like ripples in a pool of water, it spread out from her center until it touched every part of her, from the soles of her feet to her scalp. Just as relentless, his strokes grew bold. They quickened, like her breath.

She could feel the thrum of impending orgasm surfacing.

He slowed his pace again and she groaned with dissatisfaction.

"What's wrong, baby?"

She didn't miss the smug satisfaction in his voice. "You're a cruel bastard, that's what. You're enjoying torturing me, aren't you?"

"Torture?" The surprise in his voice sounded genuine and if she hadn't known that years ago he'd been recognized as a talented actor in college, she might have believed it. "Is that what you think I'm doing?" His intimate strokes stopped and it was only then that she realized what true torture was. The absence of his touch made her want to cry out, nearby diners or not. "Have you had enough?"

"Not by a long shot," she answered, not bothering to hide her frustration.

"Would you like to go home?"

"Your home. You've only whetted my appetite, you damn tease."

"Your wish is my desire." The devious sparkle in his eye didn't cease until long after he'd paid the bill and they'd left restaurant.

As they walked to the car, a strong breeze caught her flirty, lightweight skirt and sent it fluttering up away from her legs a la Marilyn Monroe. Remembering her torn panties, she dropped a hand, pressing it to one upper leg then the other to keep from flashing too much of her vitals to the unsuspecting public outside. The foam container in her other hand impeded her from using both, so she wedged it against her mound to hold down the skirt's center from lifting too high.

Another bluster of wind tested her efforts, but nothing more than a little extra leg showed...until it caught the back of her skirt. She felt the material flutter against her ass and lift. She quickly pressed it back down.

"How was your dinner?" he asked, seeming to be unaware of her current troubles.

"Fine."

"Only fine?" He slid her a sideways glance. His gaze dropped for a split second to her quickly shifting hands before returning to her face. He reached for her carryout container. "Would you like me to take that for you?"

"At the moment, I think it's the only thing keeping my skirt in place."

"Okay. Just thought I'd offer. I'd be happy to hold the skirt instead."

"I'm sure you would. But that would look ridiculous, one of your hands on my ass, the other on my mound as we walk through the parking lot. We'd probably get arrested for...indecent exposure...or something."

"No, I don't think that would be indecent exposure. But if you don't tame that wild thing," he said, motioning toward her fluttering skirt, "you could be arrested for it."

She gathered the excess width in her fist until the hem was cinched tight around her legs. "I don't know what made me think to wear this tonight."

"I like it."

"That's because it wants to fly up around my belly button."

"That does add to the allure."

"We only have a few more feet. I think I can manage. Thanks."

He shook his head. "Can't say I didn't offer."

"Nope."

They reached the car without her skirt billowing up again, and relieved, she slid into the passenger seat and rested her leftover dinner in her lap. She waited until he was behind the steering wheel and had the car started before she asked, "Just tell me, we are going back to your place to finish what you started, aren't we?"

"Absolutely." He shifted the car into drive. "Hold on! It's going to be a bumpy ride."

Fond of that analogy, and hoping it would be a bumpy ride indeed, she grinned and grabbed the armrest.

# Chapter Six

ಐ

The instant they stepped into his house, she found herself wedged between Adam's considerable bulk and the wall. It was a pleasant place to be, especially considering where his hands were—cupped under her ass.

She wrapped her legs around his waist as he lifted her and let her head fall to the side as he hungrily bit and sucked her neck. He had lost control quite suddenly, the abrupt intensity of his passion catching her by surprise. Shivers and goose bumps spanned her arms, shoulders and spine and heat gathered between her legs. She let loose a moan as his tongue plunged in and out of her ear.

Her breasts were pressed flat against his chest, her pussy grinding against his stomach. She nuzzled the crook of his neck and inhaled his scent. Her tongue darted out for a quick taste. Salty. Male. A low grumble reverberated in her belly.

As he turned and walked across the living room, she locked her ankles together and clung to him. His fingers dug into the flesh of her ass and she raked her nails down his arms. He bit her neck until it stung but the pain only magnified the passion building inside of her. They bounced off the narrow hallway's walls as he carried her toward his bedroom. His arms were trembling and she realized hers were too. Outside of his room, their quick breaths came in unison as their mouths found each other and their tongues whirled and tasted and stroked.

He pushed the door open with a hip and gently laid her back on the bed. Then he paused for a moment, looking out of breath and on the verge of completely losing control…or crying.

"Are you okay?" she asked, raising herself on her elbows.

"Yeah. I'm fine, Angel."

His voice lacked any conviction, spurring her to ask, "What is it?"

He lowered himself over top of her and gently cradled her head in his hands. His mouth claimed hers, but it wasn't with the same urgent hunger it had earlier. His kiss was soft and gentle. A caress. A nip. His tongue dipped inside her mouth to taste her. She heard her words, trapped in his mouth, echo in her own, "I...love you, Adam."

His fingers tangled in her hair and tugged slightly, the sting a contrast to the painfully gentle kiss. Then he released the strands, palmed her cheeks and looked into her eyes. In his, she witnessed a mire of emotions she couldn't quite read.

"I can't," he whispered.

"Can't what?" Uh-oh. Something was wrong. Really wrong.

"I need to tell you something. Now. Before this goes any further." He pushed himself up and stood. The fingers that had been tangled in her hair raked through his. "I can't do this to you anymore."

"Do what?" Alarms going off in her head, she tugged on her skirt hem and smoothed it down over her legs. "You've been acting funny all night."

"I know. I've been trying to pretend it wasn't bothering me, but I can't pretend any longer." He drew in a breath that broadened his already enormous chest. "I lied to you."

She felt the familiar sting in her gut. He'd spoken those words to her before and they'd led to the most wrenching day of her life. How could she have been so stupid to trust him again? How could she have let her guard down so easily? "About what?"

"The book."

That wasn't what she'd expected him to say. Confused, she said, "Huh?"

"I wrote that book just to get to you. The publisher is phony. I own the company. I never intended to distribute that book. I sent only one advance copy for review. To you."

"To accomplish what? To get me into bed?" She didn't know how to feel. Confusion, anger, frustration, sorrow, they all battled for control of her racing heart.

"Kind of, but not exactly."

"You're not making much sense."

"I know."

She grabbed a pillow and hugged it to her chest. "What exactly were you hoping to gain by this?"

He sat next to her. "You. All I wanted was you."

Not sure if she should believe him, and not exactly understanding how she felt about what she was hearing, she studied his face for something, some sign that what he was saying was true.

"I didn't know how else to do this. It was sneaky, I know. Underhanded. Low."

"That crappy book was a hoax?"

He nodded dolefully. "Yeah."

"Well, I guess that part's a relief. Although after all this so-called research, I kind of believe it."

"I love you, Lara," he confessed, palming her cheek. His thumb traced her lower lip. "I've loved you for years but I didn't expect you to believe me. So I thought if I could just get you to trust me again—"

"By lying? Again?"

"It doesn't make much sense, does it?"

"No. Not really. Why not just come to me and tell me how you felt?"

"I was afraid you'd laugh in my face. You have a lot of pride. I knew you wouldn't give me a chance, not after what I'd done to you. And I can't say I blame you. I was a first-rate idiot back in college."

"I was thinking more 'heartless bastard'."

"That too. I knew how you felt about me but I was too damn busy with school to give you want you wanted — no, what you deserved. So I cut you loose, let you down as easy as I could."

"You lied, gave me the lamest excuse I've ever heard. Some bull about your parents' religion. I knew it was a lie. And I spent years trying to understand why you dumped me."

"I assumed you'd be fine, just run off, find another guy. You're so beautiful. It wasn't like you couldn't have any guy you wanted. I never thought I'd hurt you so bad. And I never expected to miss you so much, even after all this time."

"But you're still lying. You tricked me into sleeping with you. Do you know I lost my job? I got fired because…" She didn't finish the sentence. After all, it wasn't fair to dump the blame for her bad choices on him. She'd written that first review. She'd insisted it be published. Then she'd pressed the issue of the rebuttal. Barb was right, her heart wasn't in that job anymore. It was somewhere else, in the hands of one lying, scheming doctor. "You tricked me, hoping to get me to fall in love with you again?"

"I was hoping. But that was stupid, underhanded. That's why I couldn't make love to you now. I can't go through with this any longer. I won't hurt your feelings…again."

"I don't hate you."

He walked to the dresser, opened the top drawer, pulled out a folder and handed her an envelope. "I wrote this earlier today. In my gut I knew it would come to this tonight. Maybe it doesn't make what I did right, but it might explain it a little. Take it home and read it."

Barely able to keep from tearing the note open right there and then, she nodded. "Can I read it now?"

"Please wait until you get home. I want you to have some time to yourself, to think, fume, curse, damn me to hell, whatever." He took her hands in his and helped her to her feet. "I'll take you home now." Still looking remorseful, his sorrow

201

palpable, heavy and dark, filling the cool night air, he walked her to the car, drove her home and saw her safely inside.

She watched his red tail lights disappear into the deepening night then closed the front door and curled up in bed to read the note.

*Dear Lara,*

*They say desperate men do desperate things and that can be my only excuse for what I've done. Since shortly after our breakup in college, I haven't lived a day without regretting what I'd done to you. I made a terrible mistake but instead of being a man and living with the results of that impulsive, thoughtless action, I was a complete ass and decided to trick you into reconciling with me. I suppose I never expected it to work and that's why I suddenly found myself up all night, pacing the floor with guilt. When you said you loved me, I struggled with the decision to tell you the truth. But I was too weak and spineless...until now.*

*I am saddened by the thought that you could tell me to take a flying leap off the Ambassador Bridge, but at the same time I'm relieved to finally have the truth revealed. If nothing else, this may prove to you that I would do anything to have you in my life, including make you hate me.*

*Am I a pathetic man? Or just a man pathetically in love?*

*I won't call you, despite the fact that I have your phone number programmed under ten different quick dial codes. I won't visit your house, despite the fact that I could drive there in my sleep, the route is so ingrained. I won't even read your newspaper column, despite the fact that I've collected every one of them since your first one, eight years ago.*

*What happens next is entirely up to you.*

*Love always, Adam.*

Lara dropped the note on her bed and cried herself to sleep.

The next morning, she read the note at least a couple dozen times and each time, she felt a little less angry. Yes, he'd been unforgivably sneaky. But she knew why. He was right. Her pride never would have allowed her to accept the truth, no matter how many times he might have told her. In a crazy way, he'd risked a great deal to prove the depth of his feelings for her. No man had ever done such a thing before.

He loved her.

Now, she had a choice to make. What would she do about it? Would she do the safest thing and walk away, assuming he would trick her and lie to her again? As much as her head told her that was the best route to follow, her heart wouldn't allow it.

Would she go to him and tell him how she felt? That was almost too easy, considering the lengths he'd gone to get her back.

She needed to *do* something.

An insane idea struck and although she probably should dismiss it immediately, she entertained it instead. And then she acted upon it, picking up the phone to call someone she'd met only once at a writer's conference in Ohio.

She was in her office.

A quick phone call, a short fax, and the deal was sealed.

Now it was time to dress and go tell Adam. He would be floored! She couldn't wait to see his face. She glanced at the clock. A little less than one hour from now she had to be at his place if she wanted to see his reaction.

After a quick shower, she dressed, did her hair and makeup and ran out the door. She stopped at a bagel place on the way to his house for some breakfast. Unfortunately, the deli was packed and it took longer than she expected. She ran to her car and drove just over the speed limit to his house, one eye on the road, the other on the clock.

With only minutes to spare, the brown paper bag full of bagels in one hand, a carrier with two coffees in the other, she kicked his front door.

The surprise on his face didn't hide the deep shadows and bloodshot eyes that told her he hadn't slept. Still wearing the same clothes he'd worn last night, he stepped aside to welcome her in. "Hi. What are you doing here?"

"Good morning. I brought some breakfast. I hope you haven't eaten yet."

"No..."

She glanced at the clock on his fireplace mantel.

The phone rang but he didn't move to get it.

"You'd better answer that," she said.

"No, I'll let the voicemail pick it up. I couldn't care less about a phone call right now. At this hour, it's got to be a sales call anyway."

"I wouldn't be too sure about that." She set the food and drinks down on the coffee table and shoved him toward the kitchen where the phone was. "Answer it."

"What are you up to?"

"Just answer it."

She watched as he said, "Hello?" and as surprise and shock and amusement and love washed one emotion at a time over his face as he listened to the caller.

He barely spoke two words before hanging up, and then laughing, he swept her into his arms and hugged her tightly. "You crazy, insane woman."

"You set out to prove to me that your book wasn't a pile of horseshit and you did it. And now that I believe in it, I wanted to make sure your book had a better distribution than Powers Publishing could provide. I hope you don't mind. Beth Seward is the best agent out there. I'm sure she'll get you a fantastic deal."

"You're serious?"

"Dead serious. Now that we've settled that, how about we go test a few more statistics? You have those handcuffs we talked about yesterday? I need a good workout. My favorite jeans are feeling a little snug. Not to mention you look like you could use a little sexual healing," she added, quoting the title of one of her favorite 1980s tunes.

"What about you? A job?" he asked as he hefted her over his shoulder and carried her into the bedroom. "You lost your job because of me."

"No, I lost my job because of me. Barb was right. I needed a change."

"Well, I have a position you might be interested in." He lowered her to the bed and gazed down into her eyes...

# Epilogue

**೫**

"We have a special treat for you today," Gloria Day, hostess of the morning drive time program on WDYH Talk Radio, said into her microphone. "With me this morning are Dr. Adam Roy and his lovely wife and coauthor, Lara Roy, to talk about their recent book release, a sequel to Dr. Roy's *The Sex Plan*. Welcome Dr. Roy, Mrs. Roy."

"Good to be here," Lara said stiffly, trying hard not to sound or look as nervous as she felt. She shifted uncomfortably on the padded bench and almost knocked her forehead into the microphone positioned mere inches from her face. "Oops."

Adam, sitting next to her, gave her hand a gentle squeeze of encouragement. "Good morning, Detroit!" he said in his practiced Robin Williams voice.

Lara rolled her eyes.

Gloria deadpanned him.

"Sorry. I've always wanted to do that," Adam said, not looking sorry in the least, which made Lara laugh. She swallowed her giggles, not wanting them to be caught by the microphone. She was knocking into the equipment, and he was slaughtering lines from an old movie. Not the professional image she was hoping for. Oh well.

"Yessss… So, let's talk about your book, shall we? The title is intriguing. *The Love Plan.* Dr. Roy, would you care to give us a little information about the book? What made you, a medical doctor, decide to write a book about relationships?"

"That's an easy one." He grinned at Lara. "My wife."

Lara smiled.

"How very sweet. Your wife inspired you?" Gloria asked.

"Oh no. She threatened me with bodily harm," Adam said without so much as a blink.

"Adam. I did not," Lara blurted, forgetting for a moment about the gazillion of people sitting in their cars, listening to their conversation. But she was quickly reminded when she looked over Adam's shoulder at the crowd of people gathering at the wide window behind him, staring in at her. Why, oh why, had she let Adam talk her into doing this interview? They'd come to an understanding a long time ago. He was the media maven. She was the silent partner, the brains behind Adam's beauty.

Adam nodded. "Sure you did. Don't you remember? It went along the lines of 'You'd better write that book or I'm going to kick your a—'"

"Adam!" Lara interrupted, trying not to crack up. "You can't say those words on the radio."

"What? Why not?" Adam asked. He turned to Gloria. "What's his face—the guy with the long hair—says worse than that...er, not that I listen to him."

"He's on late at night—when the kiddies are not munching on dry cereal in their car seats while mom drives them to daycare," Lara explained, fighting a wave of woozy nausea. The past few weeks had been rough. Morning sickness, ha! Not for her. It was all-day sickness, twenty-four, seven. She needed a soda cracker. Pronto. She wondered if the crunching would be distracting.

"Ah. Sorry." Adam said with an understanding nod. "Luckily for the unsuspecting listeners my wife has a quick tongue."

"No, I'd say you're the lucky one, Dr. Roy," Gloria said.

Lara felt her cheeks heating, and not because of the nausea. "Back to the book." Swallowing against the urge to gag, she gave Adam her best thanks-for-nothing glare. As usual, he answered with a bat of his eyelashes and his innocent puppy dog face. She was always a sucker for the puppy dog face. "My husband's first book, *The Sex Plan*, was a huge success."

"Thanks to my wife," Adam added.

"But I felt he owed his readers the follow-up," Lara continued. "In that first book, he'd only told the beginning of the story. Sex does produce positive health results, but so does being in a healthy, stable relationship. It's especially beneficial for men." She made sure to emphasize those last two words. She reached down for her purse and oh- so carefully extracted a soda cracker from it.

"Yes," Gloria agreed. "And since your book's release, there's been a statistically significant increase in the number of marriages across the country, as well as a new interest in classes, workshops and counseling services all meant to build marriages."

"We honestly didn't expect it to receive this kind of reaction," Adam said, winking at Lara. He blew her a kiss and mouthed the words, "I love you."

Lara chewed her cracker as quietly as possible, swallowed and mouthed back, "I love you to. Behave yourself."

He pouted. She resisted the urge to give him a playful pinch and blew him a kiss instead, blowing a few cracker crumbs with it.

"I wonder what's next for you two?" Gloria, who didn't appear to have an aversion to flying, slightly-used cracker crumbs, asked. She seemed amused as her gaze ping-ponged back and forth, following their gestures. "Do you have any plans on coauthoring any more books?"

"Why yes, we do," Adam answered. "It's called *The Baby Plan*. We're in the," he cleared his throat, "research stage at present." He winked at Lara again. Just to clarify, in case Gloria wasn't following, he patted Lara's still flat tummy as Lara wolfed down a couple more crackers.

Gloria's eyes widened. So did her smile. "Oh, how wonderful! About the book and the other good news. When are you due, Mrs. Roy?"

She swallowed hard. Dry crackers got a little pasty without some nice cold water to wash them down. "I have eight more months of…research…to go," she answered, using two fingers of both hands to gesture quotations as she said the word research.

"The effects of pregnancy on a woman's body are incredible," Adam said gleefully.

"Yes, only my husband would find a bright side to a condition that causes nonstop vomiting, exhaustion, mood swings and stretch marks," Lara muttered as another wave of nausea twisted her insides, despite the crackers she'd downed.

Gloria chuckled.

"Among other benefits, there's increased sexual pleasure, thanks to an increase in circulation to…" He hesitated for an instant, looking at Gloria for guidance as he mouthed, "vagina". She shook her head. "…certain parts of a woman's anatomy. In addition, many women adopt healthier lifestyles that remain with them after childbirth, they find long-term relief from menstrual cramps, and enjoy reduced risk of ovarian and breast cancers."

"Makes you want to go out and get pregnant this very instant, doesn't it?" Gloria joked.

"Ha!" Lara blurted. She cleared her throat. "I mean, not hardly. But it does make suffering all the not-so-pleasant effects a little easier."

"I also happen to think all the changes in pregnancy, the thicker hair and softer body, make a woman extremely attractive," Adam added, giving Lara a lustful smile. "I'm still gathering data but I've had some very surprising findings. Unfortunately, it may take more than one pregnancy to collect all the information I need."

"Sounds like you're in for a large family." Gloria grinned then patted Lara's shoulder in sympathy.

"Oh, no we're not." Lara, who was sure her face was the hue of moss, gave her randy husband the evil eye. "Unless I start feeling better, like today, Dr. Roy can gather data from other pregnant women. I agreed to be his guinea pig once but if I'm going to feel like this for almost ten months, I'm not volunteering for a repeat performance."

"We'll see," Adam said. "We still have a lifetime's worth of topics to research. Despite my wife's strong words, she's an eager research assistant. Mainly because I make sure there's adequate compensation—"

"Adam!" Lara glanced at the people watching through the window. They were all practically doubled over with laughter. "I'll get you for that," she mumbled, smiling.

"What's that, dear?" he asked, donning his most convincing I'm-innocent expression. Oh yeah, he'd heard her all right.

"I said, yes, dear. I've had some ideas for future projects myself. Like the health benefits of hard physical labor...or sleeping on the couch...or abstaining from watching sports on television." For that last one, she received a high five from Gloria.

"It sounds like we have lots to look forward to from this intelligent, successful couple," Gloria said.

"Yes," Lara agreed triumphantly as she sank into Adam's warm embrace. "Lots and lots and lots."

*The End*

# Also by Tawny Taylor

ॐ

Body and Soul: Pesky Paranormals
Body and Soul: Phantasmic Fantasies
Ellora's Cavemen: Tales From the Temple IV (*anthology*)
Immortal Secrets 1: Dragons and Dungeons
Immortal Secrets 2: Light My Fire
Immortal Secrets 3: Spells and Seduction
Passion and a Pear Tree
Private Games
Siren's Dance
Stolen Goddess
Tempting Fate
Wet and Wilde

# About the Author

Nothing exciting happens in Tawny Taylor's life, unless you count giving the cat a flea dip—a cat can make some fascinating sounds when immersed chin-deep in insecticide—or chasing after a houseful of upchucking kids during flu season. She doesn't travel the world or employ a staff of personal servants. She's not even built like a runway model. She's just your run-of-the-mill, pleasantly plump Detroit suburban mom and wife.

That's why she writes, for the sheer joy of it. She doesn't need to escape, mind you. Despite being run-of-the-mill, her life is wonderful. She just likes to add some...zip.

Her heroines might resemble herself, or her next door neighbor (sorry Sue), but they are sure to be memorable (she hopes!). And her heroes—inspired by movie stars, her favorite television actors or her husband—are fully capable of delivering one hot happily-ever-after after another. Combined, the characters and plots she weaves bring countless hours of enjoyment to Tawny...and she hopes to readers too!

In the end, that's all the matters to Tawny, bringing a little bit of zip to someone else's life.

Tawny welcomes comments from readers. You can find her website and email address on her author bio page at www.ellorascave.com

*Enjoy An Excerpt From:*

# ABOUT MONDAY

## Available at www.cerridwenpress.com

Even semi-asleep, Jenny sensed something was different. The bed felt unfamiliar, softer, and it smelled like perfume. The scent burned her nose.

As she drifted closer to complete wakefulness, she realized there was no traffic noise rumbling through the open window. No trucks roaring down the freeway or angry motorists on the verge of morning rush-hour road-rage blaring their horns. It was peaceful. Serene.

What the heck? Was the freeway shut down?

She blinked and opened her eyes and immediately realized why she didn't hear the traffic and why the bed felt different.

This wasn't her bed or her bedroom. Where the hell was she?

Her heart immediately shifting into triple-pace as panic wound its way around her insides and clamped down tight, she sat up and looked around the room. It was a fancy place. All the furniture matched. The bed, a massive dark wood piece of furniture with a gorgeous brocade canopy surrounding it, sat positioned in the middle of one wall. The window, dressed in curtains to match the canopy, was directly opposite.

She ran across the room, not completely unaware of how soft the carpet felt under her bare feet, and pulled the curtain aside. She stared into a lush green lawn full of mature trees.

No clues there.

Turning slowly, she scanned the room again for a sign of where she was. Why would anyone kidnap her and bring her to a place like this? It made absolutely no sense.

She ran to the door and gripped the knob, fully expecting it to be locked. It turned without a problem.

Why would someone kidnap her and put her in an unlocked room? Had to be the dumbest kidnappers in history. She opened the door just enough to poke her head out and took a peek. There wasn't an armed guard standing in the hallway.

*Weird. Gotta do some more investigating but I need to take care of one minor problem first.*

Feeling like her bladder was about ready to burst, she spun around, pushing the door closed as she turned. But as she took a step forward, something caught, yanking her backward.

Her nightgown was trapped in the door. She opened it, pulled the filmy material free, closed it again and…*nightgown?*…and freaked out!

Someone had changed her clothes? Where were her sweats and T-shirt?

Exactly how far down had they undressed her? Surely they hadn't stripped her nude, had they?

*How embarrassing. I wasn't wearing my good underwear last night.* She untied the lace at her throat and peered straight down. Yikes! She had no underwear or bra on.

*Sheesh, with boobs like that I don't need a bra…*

*Wait a minute! Oh God!*

"There is a boob fairy!" she said to the air before looking down to admire her new breasts again. "I was expecting you about fifteen years ago, but I suppose it's better late than never." Those had to be at least thirty-four C's or maybe D's. She'd never seen anything that large up close and personal. Up until now she'd been blessed with barely-there thirty-two A's.

Someone kidnapped her, gave her plastic surgery and then brought her to this fancy place to recover? Funny, she didn't feel a twinge of pain. Her friend Janice got a boob job and moaned about the pain for months. Wimp.

Yippee! What rich fairy godmother did she have to thank for this? Or was it one of those reality shows? Was there a hidden camera in the room somewhere? She nervously glanced around, eyeing artwork on the wall with suspicion. Maybe it was hidden behind that busy floral print over there… *It's too ugly to be there for any other reason.* She walked over to get a better look.

Didn't seem to be any peepholes for tiny camera lenses. No, the reality show idea was losing credibility quickly.

The fairy godmother theory was too—at least a real human fairy godmother—since it couldn't be legal to perform plastic surgery on someone without their knowledge or consent.

That left her with no logical explanations. This was getting stranger by the second.

Now, hardly able to catch her breath, thanks to equal doses of confusion and panic, as well as a spasming bladder, Jenny ran across the room and tried a door that looked like it might lead to a bathroom.

As she found herself in the middle of a well-stocked, walk-in closet, she realized her bladder wasn't the only part of her in an uproar. Her empty stomach was clenching and unclenching and she was about to retch.

Luckily, the second door she tried led to a bathroom. She dashed inside, grabbed an empty trash can to catch anything coming up, yanked up her nightgown and sat on the toilet to catch anything going down. And settled in for the long haul.

When she finally had herself collected, she stood up and looked into the mirror to see if anything else had been surgically altered…

…and nearly fell over.

Her hands gripping the smooth polished stone countertop, she screamed, "Oh my God!" One hand rose to her face, her fingertips searching the lines and curves of familiar features, but ones that definitely didn't belong to her.

"I'm…Monica? But how?" Even her voice sounded different. Could a surgeon change a person's voice?

Immediately she recalled last night's wish but dismissed it. That was a silly, childish rhyme, not magic. Real magic didn't exist outside of fairy-tales and movies, everyone knew that. Those fancy magicians who made DC-10 airplanes disappear used illusion.

This had to be some kind of illusion too.

She pulled her hair back and gathered it into one fist, then felt along her hairline for some kind of seam, figuring someone had put some of that special makeup on her, like the rubber mask Robin Williams wore in that old movie, *Mrs. Doubtfire.* But after searching thoroughly, she concluded either there was no makeup or it was applied so well it couldn't be detected.

Maybe a shower would wash some of it away.

She turned on the water—no easy task, considering the number of gadgets and gizmos in the glass enclosed cubicle— and stepped inside, scrubbing from top to toe with soap. When she stepped out and scrutinized her face in the mirror, she still found no signs of makeup, no seams or smears.

Okay. Running out of steam fast, she sat on a cushy bench in front of the mirror and stared at herself. There had to be a logical explanation. Didn't there?

Whoever was responsible for this crazy event evidently wanted her to play Monica for a day or two for some reason. Why, she couldn't begin to guess. But she figured she had two options—either she could hide out until someone showed up to explain it to her, or she could make the best of it and do what she'd secretly dreamed of doing—see how it felt walking in three-inch Manolo Blahnik's and driving a Lexus.

# Why an electronic book?

We live in the Information Age—an exciting time in the history of human civilization, in which technology rules supreme and continues to progress in leaps and bounds every minute of every day. For a multitude of reasons, more and more avid literary fans are opting to purchase e-books instead of paper books. The question from those not yet initiated into the world of electronic reading is simply: *Why?*

1. ***Price.*** An electronic title at Ellora's Cave Publishing and Cerridwen Press runs anywhere from 40% to 75% less than the cover price of the exact same title in paperback format. Why? Basic mathematics and cost. It is less expensive to publish an e-book (no paper and printing, no warehousing and shipping) than it is to publish a paperback, so the savings are passed along to the consumer.

2. ***Space.*** Running out of room in your house for your books? That is one worry you will never have with electronic books. For a low one-time cost, you can purchase a handheld device specifically designed for e-reading. Many e-readers have large, convenient screens for viewing. Better yet, hundreds of titles can be stored within your new library—on a single microchip. There are a variety of e-readers from different manufacturers. You can also read e-books on your PC or laptop computer. (Please note that Ellora's

Cave does not endorse any specific brands. You can check our websites at www.ellorascave.com or www.cerridwenpress.com for information we make available to new consumers.)

3. *Mobility.* Because your new e-library consists of only a microchip within a small, easily transportable e-reader, your entire cache of books can be taken with you wherever you go.

4. *Personal Viewing Preferences.* Are the words you are currently reading too small? Too large? Too... ANNOYING? Paperback books cannot be modified according to personal preferences, but e-books can.

5. *Instant Gratification.* Is it the middle of the night and all the bookstores near you are closed? Are you tired of waiting days, sometimes weeks, for bookstores to ship the novels you bought? Ellora's Cave Publishing sells instantaneous downloads twenty-four hours a day, seven days a week, every day of the year. Our webstore is never closed. Our e-book delivery system is 100% automated, meaning your order is filled as soon as you pay for it.


Those are a few of the top reasons why electronic books are replacing paperbacks for many avid readers.

As always, Ellora's Cave and Cerridwen Press welcome your questions and comments. We invite you to email us at Comments@ellorascave.com or write to us directly at Ellora's Cave Publishing Inc., 1056 Home Avenue, Akron, OH 44310-3502.

# THE
# ☥ ELLORA'S CAVE ☥
# LIBRARY

Stay up to date with Ellora's Cave Titles in
Print with our Quarterly Catalog.

TO RECIEVE A CATALOG,
SEND AN EMAIL WITH YOUR NAME
AND MAILING ADDRESS TO:

CATALOG@ELLORASCAVE.COM
OR SEND A LETTER OR POSTCARD
WITH YOUR MAILING ADDRESS TO:

CATALOG REQUEST
C/O ELLORA'S CAVE PUBLISHING, INC.
1056 HOME AVENUE
AKRON, OHIO 44310-3502

erridwen, the Celtic Goddess of wisdom, was the muse who brought inspiration to story-tellers and those in the creative arts. Cerridwen Press encompasses the best and most innovative stories in all genres of today's fiction. Visit our site and discover the newest titles by talented authors who still get inspired - much like the ancient storytellers did, once upon a time.

# Cerridwen Press

www.cerridwenpress.com

Discover for yourself why readers can't get enough of the multiple award-winning publisher Ellora's Cave.

Whether you prefer e-books or paperbacks,

be sure to visit EC on the web at www.ellorascave.com

for an erotic reading experience that will leave you breathless.